John Galsworthy – Villa Rubein

John Galsworthy was born at Kingston Upon Thames in Surrey, England, on August 14th 1867 to a wealthy and well established family. His schooling was at Harrow and New College, Oxford before training as a barrister and being called to the bar in 1890. However, Law was not attractive to him and he travelled abroad becoming great friends with the novelist Joseph Conrad, then a first mate on a sailing ship.

In 1895 Galsworthy began an affair with Ada Nemesis Pearson Cooper, the wife of his cousin Major Arthur Galsworthy. The affair was kept a secret for 10 years till she at last divorced and they married on 23 September 1905.

Galsworthy first published in 1897 with a collection of short stories entitled "The Four Winds". For the next 7 years he published these and all works under his pen name John Sinjohn. It was only upon the death of his father and the publication of "The Island Pharisees" in 1904 that he published as John Galsworthy.

His first play, The Silver Box in 1906 was a success and was followed by "The Man of Property" later that same year and was the first in the Forsyte trilogy. Whilst today he is far more well know as a Nobel Prize winning novelist then he was considered a playwright dealing with social issues and the class system. Here we publish Villa Rubein, a very fine story that captures Galsworthy's unique narrative and take on life of the time.

He is now far better known for his novels, particularly The Forsyte Saga, his trilogy about the eponymous family of the same name. These books, as with many of his other works, deal with social class, upper-middle class lives in particular. Although always sympathetic to his characters, he reveals their insular, snobbish, and somewhat greedy attitudes and suffocating moral codes. He is now viewed as one of the first from the Edwardian era to challenge some of the ideals of society depicted in the literature of Victorian England.

In his writings he campaigns for a variety of causes, including prison reform, women's rights, animal welfare, and the opposition of censorship as well as a recurring theme of an unhappy marriage from the women's side. During World War I he worked in a hospital in France as an orderly after being passed over for military service.

He was appointed to the Order of Merit in 1929, after earlier turning down a knighthood, and awarded the Nobel Prize in 1932 though he was too ill to attend.

John Galsworthy died from a brain tumour at his London home, Grove Lodge, Hampstead on January 31st 1933. In accordance with his will he was cremated at Woking with his ashes then being scattered over the South Downs from an aeroplane.

INDEX OF CONTENTS

John Galsworthy – His Life And Times

PREFACE

Writing not long ago to my oldest literary friend, I expressed in a moment of heedless sentiment the wish that we might have again one of our talks of long-past days, over the purposes and methods of our art. And my friend, wiser than I, as he has always been, replied with this doubting phrase "Could we recapture the zest of that old time?"

I would not like to believe that our faith in the value of imaginative art has diminished, that we think it less worth while to struggle for glimpses of truth and for the words which may pass them on to other eyes; or that we can no longer discern the star we tried to follow; but I do fear, with him, that half a lifetime of endeavour has dulled the exuberance which kept one up till morning discussing the ways and means of aesthetic achievement. We have discovered, perhaps with a certain finality, that by no talk can a writer add a cubit to his stature, or change the temperament which moulds and colours the vision of life he sets before the few who will pause to look at it. And so—the rest is silence, and what of work we may still do will be done in that dogged muteness which is the lot of advancing years.

Other times, other men and modes, but not other truth. Truth, though essentially relative, like Einstein's theory, will never lose its ever-new and unique quality-perfect proportion; for Truth, to the human consciousness at least, is but that vitally just relation of part to whole which is the very condition of life itself. And the task before the imaginative writer, whether at the end of the last century or all these aeons later, is the presentation of a vision which to eye and ear and mind has the implicit proportions of Truth.

I confess to have always looked for a certain flavour in the writings of others, and craved it for my own, believing that all true vision is so coloured by the temperament of the seer, as to have not only the just proportions but the essential novelty of a living thing for, after all, no two living things are alike. A work of fiction should carry the hall mark of its author as surely as a Goya, a Daumier, a Velasquez, and a Mathew Maris, should be the unmistakable creations of those masters. This is not to speak of tricks and manners which lend themselves to that facile elf, the caricaturist, but of a certain individual way of seeing and feeling. A young poet once said of another and more popular poet: "Oh! yes, but he cuts no ice." And, when one came to think of it, he did not; a certain flabbiness of spirit, a lack of temperament, an absence, perhaps, of the ironic, or passionate, view, insubstantiated his work; it had no edge—just a felicity which passed for distinction with the crowd.

Let me not be understood to imply that a novel should be a sort of sandwich, in which the author's mood or philosophy is the slice of ham. One's demand is for a far more subtle impregnation of flavour; just that, for instance, which makes De Maupassant a more poignant and fascinating writer than his master Flaubert, Dickens and Thackeray more living and permanent than George Eliot or Trollope. It once fell to my lot to be the preliminary critic of a book on painting, designed to prove that the artist's sole function was the impersonal elucidation of the truths of nature. I was regretfully compelled to observe that there were no such things as the truths of Nature, for the purposes of art, apart from the individual vision of the artist. Seer and thing seen, inextricably involved one with the other, form the texture of any masterpiece; and I, at least, demand therefrom a distinct impression of temperament. I never saw, in the flesh, either De Maupassant or Tchekov—those masters of such different methods entirely devoid of didacticism—but their work leaves on me a strangely potent sense of personality. Such subtle intermingling of seer with thing seen is the outcome only of long and intricate brooding, a process not too favoured by modern life, yet without which we achieve little but a fluent chaos of clever insignificant impressions, a kind of glorified journalism, holding much the same relation to the deeply-impregnated work of Turgenev, Hardy, and Conrad, as a film bears to a play.

Speaking for myself, with the immodesty required of one who hazards an introduction to his own work, I was writing fiction for five years before I could master even its primary technique, much less achieve that union of seer with thing seen, which perhaps begins to show itself a little in this volume—binding up the scanty harvests of 1899, 1900, and 1901—especially in the tales: "A Knight," and "Salvation of a Forsyte." Men, women, trees, and works of fiction—very tiny are the seeds from which they spring. I used really to see the "Knight"—in 1896, was it?—sitting in the "Place" in front of the Casino at Monte Carlo; and because his dried-up elegance, his burnt straw hat, quiet courtesy of attitude, and big dog, used to fascinate and intrigue me, I began to imagine his life so as to answer my own questions and to satisfy, I suppose, the mood I was in. I never spoke to him, I never saw him again. His real story, no doubt, was as different from that which I wove around his figure as night from day.

As for Swithin, wild horses will not drag from me confession of where and when I first saw the prototype which became enlarged to his bulky stature. I owe Swithin much, for he first released the satirist in me, and is, moreover, the only one of my characters whom I killed before I gave him life, for it is in "The Man of Property" that Swithin Forsyte more memorably lives.

Ranging beyond this volume, I cannot recollect writing the first words of "The Island Pharisees"—but it would be about August, 1901. Like all the stories in "Villa Rubein," and, indeed, most of my tales, the book originated in the curiosity, philosophic reflections, and unphilosophic emotions roused in me by some single figure in real life. In this case it was Ferrand, whose real name, of course, was not Ferrand, and who died in some "sacred institution" many years ago of a consumption brought on by the conditions of his wandering life. If not "a beloved," he was a true vagabond, and I first met him in the Champs Elysees, just as in "The Pigeon" he describes his meeting with Wellwyn. Though drawn very much from life, he did not in the end turn out very like the Ferrand of real life—the figures of fiction soon diverge from their prototypes.

The first draft of "The Island Pharisees" was buried in a drawer; when retrieved the other day, after nineteen years, it disclosed a picaresque string of anecdotes told by Ferrand in the first person. These two-thirds of a book were laid to rest by Edward Garnett's dictum that its author was not sufficiently within Ferrand's skin; and, struggling heavily with laziness and pride, he started afresh in the skin of Shelton. Three times be wrote that novel, and then it was long in finding the eye of Sydney Pawling, who accepted it for Heinemann's in 1904. That was a period of ferment and transition with me, a kind of long awakening to the home truths of social existence and national character. The liquor bubbled too furiously for clear bottling. And the book, after all, became but an introduction to all those following novels which depict—somewhat satirically—the various sections of English "Society" with a more or less capital "S."

Looking back on the long-stretched-out body of one's work, it is interesting to mark the endless duel fought within a man between the emotional and critical sides of his nature, first one, then the other, getting the upper hand, and too seldom fusing till the result has the mellowness of full achievement. One can even tell the nature of one's readers, by their preference for the work which reveals more of this side than of that. My early work was certainly more emotional than critical. But from 1901 came nine years when the critical was, in the main, holding sway. From 1910 to 1918 the emotional again struggled for the upper hand; and from that time on there seems to have been something of a "dead beat." So the conflict goes, by what mysterious tides promoted, I know not.

An author must ever wish to discover a hapless member of the Public who, never yet having read a word of his writing, would submit to the ordeal of reading him right through from beginning to end. Probably the effect could only be judged through an autopsy, but in the remote case of survival, it would interest one so profoundly to see the differences, if any, produced in that reader's character or outlook over life. This, however, is a consummation which will remain devoutly to be wished, for there is a limit to human complaisance. One will never know the exact measure of one's infecting power; or whether, indeed, one is not just a long soporific.

A writer they say, should not favouritize among his creations; but then a writer should not do so many things that he does. This writer, certainly, confesses to having favourites, and of his novels so far be likes best: The Forsyte Series; "The Country House"; "Fraternity"; "The Dark Flower"; and "Five Tales"; believing these to be the works which most fully achieve fusion of seer with thing seen, most subtly disclose the individuality of their author, and best reveal such of truth as has been vouchsafed to him. JOHN GALSWORTHY.

VILLA RUBEIN

I

Walking along the river wall at Botzen, Edmund Dawney said to Alois Harz: "Would you care to know the family at that pink house, Villa Rubein?"

Harz answered with a smile:

"Perhaps."

"Come with me then this afternoon."

They had stopped before an old house with a blind, deserted look, that stood by itself on the wall; Harz pushed the door open.

"Come in, you don't want breakfast yet. I'm going to paint the river to-day."

He ran up the bare broad stairs, and Dawney followed leisurely, his thumbs hooked in the armholes of his waistcoat, and his head thrown back.

In the attic which filled the whole top story, Harz had pulled a canvas to the window. He was a young man of middle height, square shouldered, active, with an angular face, high cheek-bones, and a strong, sharp chin. His eyes were piercing and steel-blue, his eyebrows very flexible, nose long and thin with a high bridge; and his dark, unparted hair fitted him like a cap. His clothes looked as if he never gave them a second thought.

This room, which served for studio, bedroom, and sitting-room, was bare and dusty. Below the window the river in spring flood rushed down the valley, a stream, of molten bronze. Harz dodged before the canvas like a fencer finding his distance; Dawney took his seat on a packingcase.

"The snows have gone with a rush this year," he drawled. "The Talfer comes down brown, the Eisack comes down blue; they flow into the Etsch and make it green; a parable of the Spring for you, my painter."

Harz mixed his colours.

"I've no time for parables," he said, "no time for anything. If I could be guaranteed to live to ninety-nine, like Titian—he had a chance. Look at that poor fellow who was killed the other day! All that struggle, and then—just at the turn!"

He spoke English with a foreign accent; his voice was rather harsh, but his smile very kindly.

Dawney lit a cigarette.

"You painters," he said, "are better off than most of us. You can strike out your own line. Now if I choose to treat a case out of the ordinary way and the patient dies, I'm ruined."

"My dear Doctor—if I don't paint what the public likes, I starve; all the same I'm going to paint in my own way; in the end I shall come out on top."

"It pays to work in the groove, my friend, until you've made your name; after that—do what you like, they'll lick your boots all the same."

"Ah, you don't love your work."

Dawney answered slowly: "Never so happy as when my hands are full. But I want to make money, to get known, to have a good time, good cigars, good wine. I hate discomfort. No, my boy, I must work it on the usual lines; I don't like it, but I must lump it. One starts in life with some notion of the ideal—it's gone by the board with me. I've got to shove along until I've made my name, and then, my little man—then—"

"Then you'll be soft!"

"You pay dearly for that first period!"

"Take my chance of that; there's no other way."

"Make one!"

"Humph!"

Harz poised his brush, as though it were a spear:

"A man must do the best in him. If he has to suffer—let him!"

Dawney stretched his large soft body; a calculating look had come into his eyes.

"You're a tough little man!" he said.

"I've had to be tough."

Dawney rose; tobacco smoke was wreathed round his unruffled hair.

"Touching Villa Rubein," he said, "shall I call for you? It's a mixed household, English mostly—very decent people."

"No, thank you. I shall be painting all day. Haven't time to know the sort of people who expect one to change one's clothes."

"As you like; ta-to!" And, puffing out his chest, Dawney vanished through a blanket looped across the doorway.

Harz set a pot of coffee on a spirit-lamp, and cut himself some bread. Through the window the freshness of the morning came; the scent of sap and blossom and young leaves; the scent of earth, and the mountains freed from winter; the new flights and songs of birds; all the odorous, enchanted, restless Spring.

There suddenly appeared through the doorway a white rough-haired terrier dog, black-marked about the face, with shaggy tan eyebrows. He sniffed at Harz, showed the whites round his eyes, and uttered a sharp bark. A young voice called:

"Scruff! Thou naughty dog!" Light footsteps were heard on the stairs; from the distance a thin, high voice called:

"Greta! You mustn't go up there!"

A little girl of twelve, with long fair hair under a wide-brimmed hat, slipped in.

Her blue eyes opened wide, her face flushed up. That face was not regular; its cheek-bones were rather prominent, the nose was flattish; there was about it an air, innocent, reflecting, quizzical, shy.

"Oh!" she said.

Harz smiled: "Good-morning! This your dog?"

She did not answer, but looked at him with soft bewilderment; then running to the dog seized him by the collar.

"Scr-ruff! Thou naughty dog—the baddest dog!" The ends of her hair fell about him; she looked up at Harz, who said:

"Not at all! Let me give him some bread."

"Oh no! You must not—I will beat him—and tell him he is bad; then he shall not do such things again. Now he is sulky; he looks so always when he is sulky. Is this your home?"

"For the present; I am a visitor."

"But I think you are of this country, because you speak like it."

"Certainly, I am a Tyroler."

"I have to talk English this morning, but I do not like it very much—because, also I am half Austrian, and I like it best; but my sister, Christian, is all English. Here is Miss Naylor; she shall be very angry with me."

And pointing to the entrance with a rosy-tipped forefinger, she again looked ruefully at Harz.

There came into the room with a walk like the hopping of a bird an elderly, small lady, in a grey serge dress, with narrow bands of claret-coloured velveteen; a large gold cross dangled from a steel chain on her chest; she nervously twisted her hands, clad in black kid gloves, rather white about the seams.

Her hair was prematurely grey; her quick eyes brown; her mouth twisted at one corner; she held her face, kind-looking, but long and narrow, rather to one side, and wore on it a look of apology. Her quick sentences sounded as if she kept them on strings, and wanted to draw them back as soon as she had let them forth.

"Greta, how can, you do such things? I don't know what your father would say! I am sure I don't know how to—so extraordinary—"

"Please!" said Harz.

"You must come at once—so very sorry—so awkward!" They were standing in a ring: Harz with his eyebrows working up and down; the little lady fidgeting her parasol; Greta, flushed and pouting, her eyes all dewy, twisting an end of fair hair round her finger.

"Oh, look!" The coffee had boiled over. Little brown streams trickled spluttering from the pan; the dog, with ears laid back and tail tucked in, went scurrying round the room. A feeling of fellowship fell on them at once.

"Along the wall is our favourite walk, and Scruff—so awkward, so unfortunate—we did not think any one lived here—the shutters are cracked, the paint is peeling off so dreadfully. Have you been long in Botzen? Two months? Fancy! You are not English? You are Tyrolese? But you speak English so well—there for seven years? Really? So fortunate!—It is Greta's day for English."

Miss Naylor's eyes darted bewildered glances at the roof where the crossing of the beams made such deep shadows; at the litter of brushes, tools, knives, and colours on a table made out of packing-cases; at the big window, innocent of glass, and flush with the floor, whence dangled a bit of rusty chain—relic of the time when the place had been a store-loft; her eyes were hastily averted from an unfinished figure of the nude.

Greta, with feet crossed, sat on a coloured blanket, dabbling her finger in a little pool of coffee, and gazing up at Harz. And he thought: 'I should like to paint her like that. "A forget-me-not."'

He took out his chalks to make a sketch of her.

"Shall you show me?" cried out Greta, scrambling to her feet.

"'Will,' Greta—'will'; how often must I tell you? I think we should be going—it is very late—your father—so very kind of you, but I think we should be going. Scruff!" Miss Naylor gave the floor two taps. The terrier backed into a plaster cast which came down on his tail, and sent him flying through the doorway. Greta followed swiftly, crying:

"Ach! poor Scrufee!"

Miss Naylor crossed the room; bowing, she murmured an apology, and also disappeared.

Harz was left alone, his guests were gone; the little girl with the fair hair and the eyes like forget-me-nots, the little lady with kindly gestures and bird-like walk, the terrier. He looked round him; the room seemed very empty. Gnawing his moustache, he muttered at the fallen cast.

Then taking up his brush, stood before his picture, smiling and frowning. Soon he had forgotten it all in his work.

II

It was early morning four days later, and Harz was loitering homewards. The shadows of the clouds passing across the vines were vanishing over the jumbled roofs and green-topped spires of the town. A strong sweet wind was blowing from the mountains, there was a stir in the branches of the trees, and flakes of the late blossom were drifting down. Amongst the soft green pods of a kind of poplar chafers buzzed, and numbers of their little brown bodies were strewn on the path.

He passed a bench where a girl sat sketching. A puff of wind whirled her drawing to the ground; Harz ran to pick it up. She took it from him with a bow; but, as he turned away, she tore the sketch across.

"Ah!" he said; "why did you do that?"

This girl, who stood with a bit of the torn sketch in either hand, was slight and straight; and her face earnest and serene. She gazed at Harz with large, clear, greenish eyes; her lips and chin were defiant, her forehead tranquil.

"I don't like it."

"Will you let me look at it? I am a painter."

"It isn't worth looking at, but—if you wish—"

He put the two halves of the sketch together.

"You see!" she said at last; "I told you."

Harz did not answer, still looking at the sketch. The girl frowned.

Harz asked her suddenly:

"Why do you paint?"

She coloured, and said:

"Show me what is wrong."

"I cannot show you what is wrong, there is nothing wrong—but why do you paint?"

"I don't understand."

Harz shrugged his shoulders.

"You've no business to do that," said the girl in a hurt voice; "I want to know."

"Your heart is not in it," said Harz.

She looked at him, startled; her eyes had grown thoughtful.

"I suppose that is it. There are so many other things—"

"There should be nothing else," said Harz.

She broke in: "I don't want always to be thinking of myself. Suppose—"

"Ah! When you begin supposing!"

The girl confronted him; she had torn the sketch again.

"You mean that if it does not matter enough, one had better not do it at all. I don't know if you are right—I think you are."

There was the sound of a nervous cough, and Harz saw behind him his three visitors—Miss Naylor offering him her hand; Greta, flushed, with a bunch of wild flowers, staring intently in his face; and the terrier, sniffing at his trousers.

Miss Naylor broke an awkward silence.

"We wondered if you would still be here, Christian. I am sorry to interrupt you—I was not aware that you knew Mr. Herr—"

"Harz is my name—we were just talking"

"About my sketch. Oh, Greta, you do tickle! Will you come and have breakfast with us to-day, Herr Harz? It's our turn, you know."

Harz, glancing at his dusty clothes, excused himself.

But Greta in a pleading voice said: "Oh! do come! Scruff likes you. It is so dull when there is nobody for breakfast but ourselves."

Miss Naylor's mouth began to twist. Harz hurriedly broke in:

"Thank you. I will come with pleasure; you don't mind my being dirty?"

"Oh no! we do not mind; then we shall none of us wash, and afterwards I shall show you my rabbits."

Miss Naylor, moving from foot to foot, like a bird on its perch, exclaimed:

"I hope you won't regret it, not a very good meal—the girls are so impulsive—such informal invitation; we shall be very glad."

But Greta pulled softly at her sister's sleeve, and Christian, gathering her things, led the way.

Harz followed in amazement; nothing of this kind had come into his life before. He kept shyly glancing at the girls; and, noting the speculative innocence in Greta's eyes, he smiled. They soon came to two great poplar-trees, which stood, like sentinels, one on either side of an unweeded gravel walk leading through lilac bushes to a house painted dull pink, with green-shuttered windows, and a roof of greenish slate. Over the door in faded crimson letters were written the words, "Villa Rubein."

"That is to the stables," said Greta, pointing down a path, where some pigeons were sunning themselves on a wall. "Uncle Nic keeps his horses there: Countess and Cuckoo—his horses begin with C, because of Chris—they are quite beautiful. He says he could drive them to Kingdom-Come and they would not turn their hair. Bow, and say 'Good-morning' to our house!"

Harz bowed.

"Father said all strangers should, and I think it brings good luck." From the doorstep she looked round at Harz, then ran into the house.

A broad, thick-set man, with stiff, brushed-up hair, a short, brown, bushy beard parted at the chin, a fresh complexion, and blue glasses across a thick nose, came out, and called in a bluff voice:

"Ha! my good dears, kiss me quick—prrt! How goes it then this morning? A good walk, hein?" The sound of many loud rapid kisses followed.

"Ha, Fraulein, good!" He became aware of Harz's figure standing in the doorway: "Und der Herr?"

Miss Naylor hurriedly explained.

"Good! An artist! Kommen Sie herein, I am delight. You will breakfast? I too—yes, yes, my dears—I too breakfast with you this morning. I have the hunter's appetite."

Harz, looking at him keenly, perceived him to be of middle height and age, stout, dressed in a loose holland jacket, a very white, starched shirt, and blue silk sash; that he looked particularly clean, had an air of belonging to Society, and exhaled a really fine aroma of excellent cigars and the best hairdresser's essences.

The room they entered was long and rather bare; there was a huge map on the wall, and below it a pair of globes on crooked supports, resembling two inflated frogs erect on their hind legs. In one corner was a cottage piano, close to a writing-table heaped with books and papers; this nook, sacred to Christian, was foreign to the rest of the room, which was arranged with supernatural neatness. A table was laid for breakfast, and the sun-warmed air came in through French windows.

The meal went merrily; Herr Paul von Morawitz was never in such spirits as at table. Words streamed from him. Conversing with Harz, he talked of Art as who should say: "One does not claim to be a connoisseur—pas si bete—still, one has a little knowledge, que diable!" He recommended him a man in the town who sold cigars that were "not so very bad." He consumed porridge, ate an omelette; and bending across to Greta gave her a sounding kiss, muttering: "Kiss me quick!"—an expression he had picked up in a London music-hall, long ago, and considered chic. He asked his daughters' plans, and held out porridge to the terrier, who refused it with a sniff.

"Well," he said suddenly, looking at Miss Naylor, "here is a gentleman who has not even heard our names!"

The little lady began her introductions in a breathless voice.

"Good!" Herr Paul said, puffing out his lips: "Now we know each other!" and, brushing up the ends of his moustaches, he carried off Harz into another room, decorated with pipe-racks, prints of dancing-girls, spittoons, easy-chairs well-seasoned by cigar smoke, French novels, and newspapers.

The household at Villa Rubein was indeed of a mixed and curious nature. Cut on both floors by corridors, the Villa was divided into four divisions; each of which had its separate inhabitants, an arrangement which had come about in the following way:

When old Nicholas Treffry died, his estate, on the boundary of Cornwall, had been sold and divided up among his three surviving children—Nicholas, who was much the eldest, a partner in the well-known firm of Forsyte and Treffry, teamen, of the Strand; Constance, married to a man called Decie; and Margaret, at her father's death engaged to the curate of the parish, John Devorell, who shortly afterwards became its rector. By his marriage with Margaret Treffry the rector had one child called Christian. Soon after this he came into some property, and died, leaving it unfettered to his widow. Three years went by, and when the child was six years old, Mrs. Devorell, still young and pretty, came to live in London with her brother Nicholas. It was there that she met Paul von Morawitz—the last of an old Czech family, who had lived for many hundred years on their estates near Budweiss. Paul had been left an orphan at the age of ten, and without a solitary ancestral acre. Instead of acres, he inherited the faith that nothing was too good for a von Morawitz. In later years his savoir faire enabled him to laugh at faith, but it stayed quietly with him all the same. The absence of acres was of no great consequence, for through his mother, the daughter of a banker in Vienna, he came into a well-nursed fortune. It befitted a von Morawitz that he should go into the Cavalry, but, unshaped for soldiering, he soon left the Service; some said he had a difference with his Colonel over the quality of food provided during some manoeuvres; others that he had retired because his chargers did not fit his legs, which were, indeed, rather round.

He had an admirable appetite for pleasure; a man-about-town's life suited him. He went his genial, unreflecting, costly way in Vienna, Paris, London. He loved exclusively those towns, and boasted that he was as much at home in one as in another. He combined exuberant vitality with fastidiousness of palate, and devoted both to the acquisition of a special taste in women, weeds, and wines; above all he was blessed with a remarkable digestion. He was thirty when he met Mrs. Devorell; and she married him because he was so very different from anybody she had ever seen. People more dissimilar were never mated. To Paul—accustomed to stage doors—freshness, serene tranquillity, and obvious purity were the baits; he had run through more than half his fortune, too, and the fact that she had money was possibly not overlooked. Be that as it may, he was fond of her; his heart was soft, he developed a domestic side.

Greta was born to them after a year of marriage. The instinct of the "freeman" was, however, not dead in Paul; he became a gambler. He lost the remainder of his fortune without being greatly disturbed. When he began to lose his wife's fortune too things naturally became more difficult. Not too much remained when Nicholas Treffry stepped in, and caused his sister to settle what was left on her daughters, after providing a life-interest for herself and Paul. Losing his supplies, the good man had given up his cards. But the instinct of the "freeman" was still living in his breast; he took to drink. He was never grossly drunk, and rarely very sober. His wife sorrowed over this new passion; her health, already much enfeebled, soon broke down. The doctors sent her to the Tyrol. She seemed to benefit by this, and settled down at Botzen. The following year, when Greta was just ten, she died. It was a shock to Paul. He gave up excessive drinking; became a constant smoker, and lent full rein to his natural domesticity. He was fond of both the girls, but did not at all understand them; Greta, his own daughter, was his favourite. Villa Rubein remained their home; it was cheap and roomy. Money, since Paul became housekeeper to himself, was scarce.

About this time Mrs. Decie, his wife's sister, whose husband had died in the East, returned to England; Paul invited her to come and live with them. She had her own rooms, her own servant; the arrangement suited Paul—it was economically sound, and there was some one always there to take care of the girls. In truth he began to feel the instinct of the "freeman" rising again within him; it was pleasant to run over to Vienna now and then; to play piquet at a Club in Gries, of which he was the shining light; in a word, to go "on the tiles" a little. One could not always mourn—even if a woman were an angel; moreover, his digestion was as good as ever.

The fourth quarter of this Villa was occupied by Nicholas Treffry, whose annual sojourn out of England perpetually surprised himself. Between him and his young niece, Christian, there existed, however, a rare sympathy; one of those affections between the young and old, which, mysteriously born like everything in life, seems the only end and aim to both, till another feeling comes into the younger heart.

Since a long and dangerous illness, he had been ordered to avoid the English winter, and at the commencement of each spring he would appear at Botzen, driving his own horses by easy stages from the Italian Riviera, where he spent the coldest months. He always stayed till June before going back to his London Club, and during all that time he let no day pass without growling at foreigners, their habits, food, drink, and raiment, with a kind of big dog's growling that did nobody any harm. The illness had broken him very much; he was seventy, but looked more. He had a servant, a Luganese, named Dominique, devoted to him. Nicholas Treffry had found him overworked in an hotel, and had engaged him with the caution: "Look—here, Dominique! I swear!" To which Dominique, dark of feature, saturnine and ironical, had only replied: "Tres biens, M'sieur!"

III

Harz and his host sat in leather chairs; Herr Paul's square back was wedged into a cushion, his round legs crossed. Both were smoking, and they eyed each other furtively, as men of different stamp do when first thrown together. The young artist found his host extremely new and disconcerting; in his presence he felt both shy and awkward. Herr Paul, on the other hand, very much at ease, was thinking indolently:

'Good-looking young fellow—comes of the people, I expect, not at all the manner of the world; wonder what he talks about.'

Presently noticing that Harz was looking at a photograph, he said: "Ah! yes! that was a woman! They are not to be found in these days. She could dance, the little Coralie! Did you ever see such arms? Confess that she is beautiful, hein?"

"She has individuality," said Harz. "A fine type!"

Herr Paul blew out a cloud of smoke.

"Yes," he murmured, "she was fine all over!" He had dropped his eyeglasses, and his full brown eyes, with little crow's-feet at the corners, wandered from his visitor to his cigar.

'He'd be like a Satyr if he wasn't too clean,' thought Harz. 'Put vine leaves in his hair, paint him asleep, with his hands crossed, so!'

"When I am told a person has individuality," Herr Paul was saying in a rich and husky voice, "I generally expect boots that bulge, an umbrella of improper colour; I expect a creature of 'bad form' as they say in England; who will shave some days and some days will not shave; who sometimes smells of India-rubber, and sometimes does not smell, which is discouraging!"

"You do not approve of individuality?" said Harz shortly.

"Not if it means doing, and thinking, as those who know better do not do, or think."

"And who are those who know better?"

"Ah! my dear, you are asking me a riddle? Well, then—Society, men of birth, men of recognised position, men above eccentricity, in a word, of reputation."

Harz looked at him fixedly. "Men who haven't the courage of their own ideas, not even the courage to smell of India-rubber; men who have no desires, and so can spend all their time making themselves flat!"

Herr Paul drew out a red silk handkerchief and wiped his beard. "I assure you, my dear," he said, "it is easier to be flat; it is more respectable to be flat. Himmel! why not, then, be flat?"

"Like any common fellow?"

"Certes; like any common fellow—like me, par exemple!" Herr Paul waved his hand. When he exercised unusual tact, he always made use of a French expression.

Harz flushed. Herr Paul followed up his victory. "Come, come!" he said. "Pass me my men of repute! que diable! we are not anarchists."

"Are you sure?" said Harz.

Herr Paul twisted his moustache. "I beg your pardon," he said slowly. But at this moment the door was opened; a rumbling voice remarked: "Morning, Paul. Who's your visitor?" Harz saw a tall, bulky figure in the doorway.

"Come in,"' called out Herr Paul. "Let me present to you a new acquaintance, an artist: Herr Harz— Mr. Nicholas Treffry. Psumm bumm! All this introducing is dry work." And going to the sideboard he poured out three glasses of a light, foaming beer.

Mr. Treffry waved it from him: "Not for me," he said: "Wish I could! They won't let me look at it." And walking over, to the window with a heavy tread, which trembled like his voice, he sat down. There was something in his gait like the movements of an elephant's hind legs. He was very tall (it was said, with the customary exaggeration of family tradition, that there never had been a male Treffry under six feet in height), but now he stooped, and had grown stout. There was something at once vast and unobtrusive about his personality.

He wore a loose brown velvet jacket, and waistcoat, cut to show a soft frilled shirt and narrow black ribbon tie; a thin gold chain was looped round his neck and fastened to his fob. His heavy cheeks had folds in them like those in a bloodhound's face. He wore big, drooping, yellow-grey moustaches, which he had a habit of sucking, and a goatee beard. He had long loose ears that might almost have been said to gap. On his head there was a soft black hat, large in the brim and low in the crown. His grey eyes, heavy-lidded, twinkled under their bushy brows with a queer, kind cynicism. As a young man he had sown many a wild oat; but he had also worked and made money in business; he had, in fact, burned the candle at both ends; but he had never been unready to do his fellows a good turn. He had a passion for driving, and his reckless method of pursuing this art had caused him to be nicknamed: "The notorious Treffry."

Once, when he was driving tandem down a hill with a loose rein, the friend beside him had said: "For all the good you're doing with those reins, Treffry, you might as well throw them on the horses' necks."

"Just so," Treffry had answered. At the bottom of the hill they had gone over a wall into a potato patch. Treffry had broken several ribs; his friend had gone unharmed.

He was a great sufferer now, but, constitutionally averse to being pitied, he had a disconcerting way of humming, and this, together with the shake in his voice, and his frequent use of peculiar phrases, made the understanding of his speech depend at times on intuition rather than intelligence.

The clock began to strike eleven. Harz muttered an excuse, shook hands with his host, and bowing to his new acquaintance, went away. He caught a glimpse of Greta's face against the window, and waved his hand to her. In the road he came on Dawney, who was turning in between the poplars, with thumbs as usual hooked in the armholes of his waistcoat.

"Hallo!" the latter said.

"Doctor!" Harz answered slyly; "the Fates outwitted me, it seems."

"Serve you right," said Dawney, "for your confounded egoism! Wait here till I come out, I shan't be many minutes."

But Harz went on his way. A cart drawn by cream-coloured oxen was passing slowly towards the bridge. In front of the brushwood piled on it two peasant girls were sitting with their feet on a mat of grass—the picture of contentment.

"I'm wasting my time!" he thought. "I've done next to nothing in two months. Better get back to London! That girl will never make a painter!" She would never make a painter, but there was something in her that he could not dismiss so rapidly. She was not exactly beautiful, but she was sympathetic. The brow was pleasing, with dark-brown hair softly turned back, and eyes so straight and shining. The two sisters were very different! The little one was innocent, yet mysterious; the elder seemed as clear as crystal!

He had entered the town, where the arcaded streets exuded their peculiar pungent smell of cows and leather, wood-smoke, wine-casks, and drains. The sound of rapid wheels over the stones made him turn his head. A carriage drawn by red-roan horses was passing at a great pace. People stared at it, standing still, and looking alarmed. It swung from side to side and vanished round a corner. Harz saw Mr. Nicholas Treffry in a long, whitish dust-coat; his Italian servant, perched behind, was holding to the seat-rail, with a nervous grin on his dark face.

'Certainly,' Harz thought, 'there's no getting away from these people this morning—they are everywhere.'

In his studio he began to sort his sketches, wash his brushes, and drag out things he had accumulated during his two months' stay. He even began to fold his blanket door. But suddenly he stopped. Those two girls! Why not try? What a picture! The two heads, the sky, and leaves! Begin to-morrow! Against that window—no, better at the Villa! Call the picture—Spring...!

IV

The wind, stirring among trees and bushes, flung the young leaves skywards. The trembling of their silver linings was like the joyful flutter of a heart at good news. It was one of those Spring mornings when everything seems full of a sweet restlessness—soft clouds chasing fast across the sky; soft scents floating forth and dying; the notes of birds, now shrill and sweet, now hushed in silences; all nature striving for something, nothing at peace.

Villa Rubein withstood the influence of the day, and wore its usual look of rest and isolation. Harz sent in his card, and asked to see "der Herr." The servant, a grey-eyed, clever-looking Swiss with no hair on his face, came back saying:

"Der Herr, mein Herr, is in the Garden gone." Harz followed him.

Herr Paul, a small white flannel cap on his head, gloves on his hands, and glasses on his nose, was watering a rosebush, and humming the serenade from Faust.

This aspect of the house was very different from the other. The sun fell on it, and over a veranda creepers clung and scrambled in long scrolls. There was a lawn, with freshly mown grass; flower-beds were laid out, and at the end of an avenue of young acacias stood an arbour covered with wisteria.

In the east, mountain peaks—fingers of snow—glittered above the mist. A grave simplicity lay on that scene, on the roofs and spires, the valleys and the dreamy hillsides, with their yellow scars and purple bloom, and white cascades, like tails of grey horses swishing in the wind.

Herr Paul held out his hand: "What can we do for you?" he said.

"I have to beg a favour," replied Harz. "I wish to paint your daughters. I will bring the canvas here—they shall have no trouble. I would paint them in the garden when they have nothing else to do."

Herr Paul looked at him dubiously—ever since the previous day he had been thinking: 'Queer bird, that painter—thinks himself the devil of a swell! Looks a determined fellow too!' Now—staring in the painter's face—it seemed to him, on the whole, best if some one else refused this permission.

"With all the pleasure, my dear sir," he said. "Come, let us ask these two young ladies!" and putting down his hose, he led the way towards the arbour, thinking: 'You'll be disappointed, my young conqueror, or I'm mistaken.'

Miss Naylor and the girls were sitting in the shade, reading La Fontaine's fables. Greta, with one eye on her governess, was stealthily cutting a pig out of orange peel.

"Ah! my dear dears!" began Herr Paul, who in the presence of Miss Naylor always paraded his English. "Here is our friend, who has a very flattering request to make; he would paint you, yes— both together, alfresco, in the air, in the sunshine, with the birds, the little birds!"

Greta, gazing at Harz, gushed deep pink, and furtively showed him her pig.

Christian said: "Paint us? Oh no!"

She saw Harz looking at her, and added, slowly: "If you really wish it, I suppose we could!" then dropped her eyes.

"Ah!" said Herr Paul raising his brows till his glasses fell from his nose: "And what says Gretchen? Does she want to be handed up to posterities a little peacock along with the other little birds?"

Greta, who had continued staring at the painter, said: "Of—course—I—want—to—be."

"Prrt!" said Herr Paul, looking at Miss Naylor. The little lady indeed opened her mouth wide, but all that came forth was a tiny squeak, as sometimes happens when one is anxious to say something, and has not arranged beforehand what it shall be.

The affair seemed ended; Harz heaved a sigh of satisfaction. But Herr Paul had still a card to play.

"There is your Aunt," he said; "there are things to be considered—one must certainly inquire—so, we shall see." Kissing Greta loudly on both cheeks, he went towards the house.

"What makes you want to paint us?" Christian asked, as soon as he was gone.

"I think it very wrong," Miss Naylor blurted out.

"Why?" said Harz, frowning.

"Greta is so young—there are lessons—it is such a waste of time!"

His eyebrows twitched: "Ah! You think so!"

"I don't see why it is a waste of time," said Christian quietly; "there are lots of hours when we sit here and do nothing."

"And it is very dull," put in Greta, with a pout.

"You are rude, Greta," said Miss Naylor in a little rage, pursing her lips, and taking up her knitting.

"I think it seems always rude to speak the truth," said Greta. Miss Naylor looked at her in that concentrated manner with which she was in the habit of expressing displeasure.

But at this moment a servant came, and said that Mrs. Decie would be glad to see Herr Harz. The painter made them a stiff bow, and followed the servant to the house. Miss Naylor and the two girls watched his progress with apprehensive eyes; it was clear that he had been offended.

Crossing the veranda, and passing through an open window hung with silk curtains, Hart entered a cool dark room. This was Mrs. Decie's sanctum, where she conducted correspondence, received her visitors, read the latest literature, and sometimes, when she had bad headaches, lay for hours on the sofa, with a fan, and her eyes closed. There was a scent of sandalwood, a suggestion of the East, a kind of mystery, in here, as if things like chairs and tables were not really what they seemed, but something much less commonplace.

The visitor looked twice, to be quite sure of anything; there were many plants, bead curtains, and a deal of silverwork and china.

Mrs. Decie came forward in the slightly rustling silk which—whether in or out of fashion—always accompanied her. A tall woman, over fifty, she moved as if she had been tied together at the knees. Her face was long, with broad brows, from which her sandy-grey hair was severely waved back; she had pale eyes, and a perpetual, pale, enigmatic smile. Her complexion had been ruined by long residence in India, and might unkindly have been called fawn-coloured. She came close to Harz, keeping her eyes on his, with her head bent slightly forward.

"We are so pleased to know you," she said, speaking in a voice which had lost all ring. "It is charming to find some one in these parts who can help us to remember that there is such a thing as Art. We had Mr. C— here last autumn, such a charming fellow. He was so interested in the native customs and dresses. You are a subject painter, too, I think? Won't you sit down?"

She went on for some time, introducing painters' names, asking questions, skating round the edge of what was personal. And the young man stood before her with a curious little smile fixed on his lips. 'She wants to know whether I'm worth powder and shot,' he thought.

"You wish to paint my nieces?" Mrs. Decie said at last, leaning back on her settee.

"I wish to have that honour," Harz answered with a bow.

"And what sort of picture did you think of?"

"That," said Harz, "is in the future. I couldn't tell you." And he thought: 'Will she ask me if I get my tints in Paris, like the woman Tramper told me of?'

The perpetual pale smile on Mrs. Decie's face seemed to invite his confidence, yet to warn him that his words would be sucked in somewhere behind those broad fine brows, and carefully sorted. Mrs. Decie, indeed, was thinking: 'Interesting young man, regular Bohemian—no harm in that at his age; something Napoleonic in his face; probably has no dress clothes. Yes, should like to see more of him!' She had a fine eye for points of celebrity; his name was unfamiliar, would probably have been scouted by that famous artist Mr. C—, but she felt her instinct urging her on to know him. She was, to do her justice, one of those "lion" finders who seek the animal for pleasure, not for the glory it brings them; she had the courage of her instincts—lion-entities were indispensable to her, but she trusted to divination to secure them; nobody could foist a "lion" on her.

"It will be very nice. You will stay and have some lunch? The arrangements here are rather odd. Such a mixed household—but there is always lunch at two o'clock for any one who likes, and we all dine at seven. You would have your sittings in the afternoons, perhaps? I should so like to see your sketches. You are using the old house on the wall for studio; that is so original of you!"

Harz would not stay to lunch, but asked if he might begin work that afternoon; he left a little suffocated by the sandalwood and sympathy of this sphinx-like woman.

Walking home along the river wall, with the singing of the larks and thrushes, the rush of waters, the humming of the chafers in his ears, he felt that he would make something fine of this subject. Before his eyes the faces of the two girls continually started up, framed by the sky, with young leaves guttering against their cheeks.

V

Three days had passed since Harz began his picture, when early in the morning, Greta came from Villa Rubein along the river dyke and sat down on a bench from which the old house on the wall was visible. She had not been there long before Harz came out.

"I did not knock," said Greta, "because you would not have heard, and it is so early, so I have been waiting for you a quarter of an hour."

Selecting a rosebud, from some flowers in her hand, she handed it to him. "That is my first rosebud this year," she said; "it is for you because you are painting me. To-day I am thirteen, Herr Harz; there is not to be a sitting, because it is my birthday; but, instead, we are all going to Meran to see the play of Andreas Hofer. You are to come too, please; I am here to tell you, and the others shall be here directly."

Harz bowed: "And who are the others?"

"Christian, and Dr. Edmund, Miss Naylor, and Cousin Teresa. Her husband is ill, so she is sad, but to-day she is going to forget that. It is not good to be always sad, is it, Herr Harz?"

He laughed: "You could not be."

Greta answered gravely: "Oh yes, I could. I too am often sad. You are making fun. You are not to make fun to-day, because it is my birthday. Do you think growing up is nice, Herr Harz?"

"No, Fraulein Greta, it is better to have all the time before you."

They walked on side by side.

"I think," said Greta, "you are very much afraid of losing time. Chris says that time is nothing."

"Time is everything," responded Harz.

"She says that time is nothing, and thought is everything," Greta murmured, rubbing a rose against her cheek, "but I think you cannot have a thought unless you have the time to think it in. There are the others! Look!"

A cluster of sunshades on the bridge glowed for a moment and was lost in shadow.

"Come," said Harz, "let's join them!"

At Meran, under Schloss Tirol, people were streaming across the meadows into the open theatre. Here were tall fellows in mountain dress, with leather breeches, bare knees, and hats with eagles' feathers; here were fruit-sellers, burghers and their wives, mountebanks, actors, and every kind of visitor. The audience, packed into an enclosure of high boards, sweltered under the burning sun. Cousin Teresa, tall and thin, with hard, red cheeks, shaded her pleasant eyes with her hand.

The play began. It depicted the rising in the Tyrol of 1809: the village life, dances and yodelling; murmurings and exhortations, the warning beat of drums; then the gathering, with flintlocks, pitchforks, knives; the battle and victory; the homecoming, and festival. Then the second gathering, the roar of cannon; betrayal, capture, death. The impassive figure of the patriot Andreas Hofer always in front, black-bearded, leathern-girdled, under the blue sky, against a screen of mountains.

Harz and Christian sat behind the others. He seemed so intent on the play that she did not speak, but watched his face, rigid with a kind of cold excitement; he seemed to be transported by the life passing before them. Something of his feeling seized on her; when the play was over she too was trembling. In pushing their way out they became separated from the others.

"There's a short cut to the station here," said Christian; "let's go this way."

The path rose a little; a narrow stream crept alongside the meadow, and the hedge was spangled with wild roses. Christian kept glancing shyly at the painter. Since their meeting on the river wall her thoughts had never been at rest. This stranger, with his keen face, insistent eyes, and ceaseless energy, had roused a strange feeling in her; his words had put shape to something in her not yet expressed. She stood aside at a stile to make way for some peasant boys, dusty and rough-haired, who sang and whistled as they went by.

"I was like those boys once," said Harz.

Christian turned to him quickly. "Ah! that was why you felt the play, so much."

"It's my country up there. I was born amongst the mountains. I looked after the cows, and slept in hay-cocks, and cut the trees in winter. They used to call me a 'black sheep,' a 'loafer' in my village."

"Why?"

"Ah! why? I worked as hard as any of them. But I wanted to get away. Do you think I could have stayed there all my life?"

Christian's eyes grew eager.

"If people don't understand what it is you want to do, they always call you a loafer!" muttered Harz.

"But you did what you meant to do in spite of them," Christian said.

For herself it was so hard to finish or decide. When in the old days she told Greta stories, the latter, whose instinct was always for the definite, would say: "And what came at the end, Chris? Do finish it this morning!" but Christian never could. Her thoughts were deep, vague, dreamy, invaded by both sides of every question. Whatever she did, her needlework, her verse-making, her painting, all had its charm; but it was not always what it was intended for at the beginning. Nicholas Treffry had once said of her: "When Chris starts out to make a hat, it may turn out an altar-cloth, but you may bet it won't be a hat." It was her instinct to look for what things meant; and this took more than all her time. She knew herself better than most girls of nineteen, but it was her reason that had informed her, not her feelings. In her sheltered life, her heart had never been ruffled except by rare fits of passion—"tantrums" old Nicholas Treffry dubbed them—at what seemed to her mean or unjust.

"If I were a man," she said, "and going to be great, I should have wanted to begin at the very bottom as you did."

"Yes," said Harz quickly, "one should be able to feel everything."

She did not notice how simply he assumed that he was going to be great. He went on, a smile twisting his mouth unpleasantly beneath its dark moustache—"Not many people think like you! It's a crime not to have been born a gentleman."

"That's a sneer," said Christian; "I didn't think you would have sneered!"

"It is true. What is the use of pretending that it isn't?"

"It may be true, but it is finer not to say it!"

"By Heavens!" said Harz, striking one hand into the other, "if more truth were spoken there would not be so many shams."

Christian looked down at him from her seat on the stile.

"You are right all the same, Fraulein Christian," he added suddenly; "that's a very little business. Work is what matters, and trying to see the beauty in the world."

Christian's face changed. She understood, well enough, this craving after beauty. Slipping down from the stile, she drew a slow deep breath.

"Yes!" she said. Neither spoke for some time, then Harz said shyly:

"If you and Fraulein Greta would ever like to come and see my studio, I should be so happy. I would try and clean it up for you!"

"I should like to come. I could learn something. I want to learn."

They were both silent till the path joined the road.

"We must be in front of the others; it's nice to be in front—let's dawdle. I forgot—you never dawdle, Herr Harz."

"After a big fit of work, I can dawdle against any one; then I get another fit of work—it's like appetite."

"I'm always dawdling," answered Christian.

By the roadside a peasant woman screwed up her sun-dried face, saying in a low voice: "Please, gracious lady, help me to lift this basket!"

Christian stooped, but before she could raise it, Harz hoisted it up on his back.

"All right," he nodded; "this good lady doesn't mind."

The woman, looking very much ashamed, walked along by Christian; she kept rubbing her brown hands together, and saying; "Gracious lady, I would not have wished. It is heavy, but I would not have wished."

"I'm sure he'd rather carry it," said Christian.

They had not gone far along the road, however, before the others passed them in a carriage, and at the strange sight Miss Naylor could be seen pursing her lips; Cousin Teresa nodding pleasantly; a smile on Dawney's face; and beside him Greta, very demure. Harz began to laugh.

"What are you laughing at?" asked Christian.

"You English are so funny. You mustn't do this here, you mustn't do that there, it's like sitting in a field of nettles. If I were to walk with you without my coat, that little lady would fall off her seat." His laugh infected Christian; they reached the station feeling that they knew each other better.

The sun had dipped behind the mountains when the little train steamed down the valley. All were subdued, and Greta, with a nodding head, slept fitfully. Christian, in her corner, was looking out of the window, and Harz kept studying her profile.

He tried to see her eyes. He had remarked indeed that, whatever their expression, the brows, arched and rather wide apart, gave them a peculiar look of understanding. He thought of his picture. There was nothing in her face to seize on, it was too sympathetic, too much like light. Yet her chin was firm, almost obstinate.

The train stopped with a jerk; she looked round at him. It was as though she had said: "You are my friend."

At Villa Rubein, Herr Paul had killed the fatted calf for Greta's Fest. When the whole party were assembled, he alone remained standing; and waving his arm above the cloth, cried: "My dears! Your happiness! There are good things here—Come!" And with a sly look, the air of a conjurer producing rabbits, he whipped the cover off the soup tureen:

"Soup-turtle, fat, green fat!" He smacked his lips.

No servants were allowed, because, as Greta said to Harz:

"It is that we are to be glad this evening."

Geniality radiated from Herr Paul's countenance, mellow as a bowl of wine. He toasted everybody, exhorting them to pleasure.

Harz passed a cracker secretly behind Greta's head, and Miss Naylor, moved by a mysterious impulse, pulled it with a sort of gleeful horror; it exploded, and Greta sprang off her chair. Scruff, seeing this, appeared suddenly on the sideboard with his forelegs in a plate of soup; without moving them, he turned his head, and appeared to accuse the company of his false position. It was the signal for shrieks of laughter. Scruff made no attempt to free his forelegs; but sniffed the soup, and finding that nothing happened, began to lap it.

"Take him out! Oh! take him out!" wailed Greta, "he shall be ill!"

"Allons! Mon cher!" cried Herr Paul, "c'est magnifique, mais, vous savez, ce nest guere la guerre!" Scruff, with a wild spring, leaped past him to the ground.

"Ah!" cried Miss Naylor, "the carpet!" Fresh moans of mirth shook the table; for having tasted the wine of laughter, all wanted as much more as they could get. When Scruff and his traces were effaced, Herr Paul took a ladle in his hand.

"I have a toast," he said, waving it for silence; "a toast we will drink all together from our hearts; the toast of my little daughter, who to-day has thirteen years become; and there is also in our hearts," he continued, putting down the ladle and suddenly becoming grave, "the thought of one who is not today with us to see this joyful occasion; to her, too, in this our happiness we turn our hearts and glasses because it is her joy that we should yet be joyful. I drink to my little daughter; may God her shadow bless!"

All stood up, clinking their glasses, and drank: then, in the hush that followed, Greta, according to custom, began to sing a German carol; at the end of the fourth line she stopped, abashed.

Heir Paul blew his nose loudly, and, taking up a cap that had fallen from a cracker, put it on.

Every one followed his example, Miss Naylor attaining the distinction of a pair of donkey's ears, which she wore, after another glass of wine, with an air of sacrificing to the public good.

At the end of supper came the moment for the offering of gifts. Herr Paul had tied a handkerchief over Greta's eyes, and one by one they brought her presents. Greta, under forfeit of a kiss, was bound to tell the giver by the feel of the gift. Her swift, supple little hands explored noiselessly; and in every case she guessed right.

Dawney's present, a kitten, made a scene by clawing at her hair.

"That is Dr. Edmund's," she cried at once. Christian saw that Harz had disappeared, but suddenly he came back breathless, and took his place at the end of the rank of givers.

Advancing on tiptoe, he put his present into Greta's hands. It was a small bronze copy of a Donatello statue.

"Oh, Herr Harz!" cried Greta; "I saw it in the studio that day. It stood on the table, and it is lovely."

Mrs. Decie, thrusting her pale eyes close to it, murmured: "Charming!"

Mr. Treffry took it in his forgers.

"Rum little toad! Cost a pot of money, I expect!" He eyed Harz doubtfully.

They went into the next room now, and Herr Paul, taking Greta's bandage, transferred it to his own eyes.

"Take care—take care, all!" he cried; "I am a devil of a catcher," and, feeling the air cautiously, he moved forward like a bear about to hug. He caught no one. Christian and Greta whisked under his arms and left him grasping at the air. Mrs. Decie slipped past with astonishing agility. Mr. Treffry, smoking his cigar, and barricaded in a corner, jeered: "Bravo, Paul! The active beggar! Can't he run! Go it, Greta!"

At last Herr Paul caught Cousin Teresa, who, fattened against the wall, lost her head, and stood uttering tiny shrieks.

Suddenly Mrs. Decie started playing The Blue Danube. Herr Paul dropped the handkerchief, twisted his moustache up fiercely, glared round the room, and seizing Greta by the waist, began dancing furiously, bobbing up and down like a cork in lumpy water. Cousin Teresa followed suit with Miss Naylor, both very solemn, and dancing quite different steps. Harz, went up to Christian.

"I can't dance," he said, "that is, I have only danced once, but—if you would try with me!"

She put her hand on his arm, and they began. She danced, light as a feather, eyes shining, feet flying, her body bent a little forward. It was not a great success at first, but as soon as the time had got into Harz's feet, they went swinging on when all the rest had stopped. Sometimes one couple or another slipped through the window to dance on the veranda, and came whirling in again. The lamplight glowed on the girls' white dresses; on Herr Paul's perspiring face. He constituted in himself a perfect orgy, and when the music stopped flung himself, full length, on the sofa gasping out:

"My God! But, my God!"

Suddenly Christian felt Harz cling to her arm.

Glowing and panting she looked at him.

"Giddy!" he murmured: "I dance so badly; but I'll soon learn."

Greta clapped her hands: "Every evening we will dance, every evening we will dance."

Harz looked at Christian; the colour had deepened in her face.

"I'll show you how they dance in my village, feet upon the ceiling!" And running to Dawney, he said:

"Hold me here! Lift me—so! Now, on—two," he tried to swing his feet above his head, but, with an "Ouch!" from Dawney, they collapsed, and sat abruptly on the floor. This untimely event brought the evening to an end. Dawney left, escorting Cousin Teresa, and Harz strode home humming The Blue Danube, still feeling Christian's waist against his arm.

In their room the two girls sat long at the window to cool themselves before undressing.

"Ah!" sighed Greta, "this is the happiest birthday I have had."

Cristian too thought: 'I have never been so happy in my life as I have been to-day. I should like every day to be like this!' And she leant out into the night, to let the air cool her cheeks.

VI

"Chris!" said Greta some days after this, "Miss Naylor danced last evening; I think she shall have a headache to-day. There is my French and my history this morning."

"Well, I can take them."

"That is nice; then we can talk. I am sorry about the headache. I shall give her some of my Eau de Cologne."

Miss Naylor's headaches after dancing were things on which to calculate. The girls carried their books into the arbour; it was a showery day, and they had to run for shelter through the raindrops and sunlight.

"The French first, Chris!" Greta liked her French, in which she was not far inferior to Christian; the lesson therefore proceeded in an admirable fashion. After one hour exactly by her watch (Mr. Treffry's birthday present loved and admired at least once every hour) Greta rose.

"Chris, I have not fed my rabbits."

"Be quick! there's not much time for history."

Greta vanished. Christian watched the bright water dripping from the roof; her lips were parted in a smile. She was thinking of something Harz had said the night before. A discussion having been started as to whether average opinion did, or did not, safeguard Society, Harz, after sitting silent, had burst out: "I think one man in earnest is better than twenty half-hearted men who follow tamely; in the end he does Society most good."

Dawney had answered: "If you had your way there would be no Society."

"I hate Society because it lives upon the weak."

"Bah!" Herr Paul chimed in; "the weak goes to the wall; that is as certain as that you and I are here."

"Let them fall against the wall," cried Harz; "don't push them there...."

Greta reappeared, walking pensively in the rain.

"Bino," she said, sighing, "has eaten too much. I remember now, I did feed them before. Must we do the history, Chris?"

"Of course!"

Greta opened her book, and put a finger in the page. "Herr Harz is very kind to me," she said. "Yesterday he brought a bird which had come into his studio with a hurt wing; he brought it very gently in his handkerchief—he is very kind, the bird was not even frightened of him. You did not know about that, Chris?"

Chris flushed a little, and said in a hurt voice

"I don't see what it has to—do with me."

"No," assented Greta.

Christian's colour deepened. "Go on with your history, Greta."

"Only," pursued Greta, "that he always tells you all about things, Chris."

"He doesn't! How can you say that!"

"I think he does, and it is because you do not make him angry. It is very easy to make him angry; you have only to think differently, and he shall be angry at once."

"You are a little cat!" said Christian; "it isn't true, at all. He hates shams, and can't bear meanness; and it is mean to cover up dislikes and pretend that you agree with people."

"Papa says that he thinks too much about himself."

"Father!" began Christian hotly; biting her lips she stopped, and turned her wrathful eyes on Greta.

"You do not always show your dislikes, Chris."

"I? What has that to do with it? Because one is a coward that doesn't make it any better, does it?"

"I think that he has a great many dislikes," murmured Greta.

"I wish you would attend to your own faults, and not pry into other people's," and pushing the book aside, Christian gazed in front of her.

Some minutes passed, then Greta leaning over, rubbed a cheek against her shoulder.

"I am very sorry, Chris—I only wanted to be talking. Shall I read some history?"

"Yes," said Christian coldly.

"Are you angry with me, Chris?"

There was no answer. The lingering raindrops pattered down on the roof. Greta pulled at her sister's sleeve.

"Look, Chris!" she said. "There is Herr Harz!"

Christian looked up, dropped her eyes again, and said: "Will you go on with the history, Greta?"

Greta sighed.

"Yes, I will—but, oh! Chris, there is the luncheon gong!" and she meekly closed the book.

During the following weeks there was a "sitting" nearly every afternoon. Miss Naylor usually attended them; the little lady was, to a certain extent, carried past objection. She had begun to take an interest in the picture, and to watch the process out of the corner of her eye; in the depths of her dear mind, however, she never quite got used to the vanity and waste of time; her lips would move and her knitting-needles click in suppressed remonstrances.

What Harz did fast he did best; if he had leisure he "saw too much," loving his work so passionately that he could never tell exactly when to stop. He hated to lay things aside, always thinking: "I can get it better." Greta was finished, but with Christian, try as he would, he was not satisfied; from day to day her face seemed to him to change, as if her soul were growing.

There were things too in her eyes that he could neither read nor reproduce.

Dawney would often stroll out to them after his daily visit, and lying on the grass, his arms crossed behind his head, and a big cigar between his lips, would gently banter everybody. Tea came at five o'clock, and then Mrs. Decie appeared armed with a magazine or novel, for she was proud of her literary knowledge. The sitting was suspended; Harz, with a cigarette, would move between the table and the picture, drinking his tea, putting a touch in here and there; he never sat down till it was all over for the day. During these "rests" there was talk, usually ending in discussion. Mrs. Decie was happiest in conversations of a literary order, making frequent use of such expressions as: "After all, it produces an illusion—does anything else matter?" "Rather a poseur, is he not?" "A question, that, of temperament," or "A matter of the definition of words"; and other charming generalities, which sound well, and seem to go far, and are pleasingly irrefutable. Sometimes the discussion turned on Art—on points of colour or technique; whether realism was quite justified; and should we be pre-Raphaelites? When these discussions started, Christian's eyes would grow bigger and clearer, with a sort of shining reasonableness; as though they were trying to see into the depths. And Harz would stare at them. But the look in those eyes eluded him, as if they had no more meaning than Mrs. Decie's, which, with their pale, watchful smile, always seemed saying: "Come, let us take a little intellectual exercise."

Greta, pulling Scruff's ears, would gaze up at the speakers; when the talk was over, she always shook herself. But if no one came to the "sittings," there would sometimes be very earnest, quick talk, sometimes long silences.

One day Christian said: "What is your religion?"

Harz finished the touch he was putting on the canvas, before he answered: "Roman Catholic, I suppose; I was baptised in that Church."

"I didn't mean that. Do you believe in a future life?"

"Christian," murmured Greta, who was plaiting blades of grass, "shall always want to know what people think about a future life; that is so funny!"

"How can I tell?" said Harz; "I've never really thought of it—never had the time."

"How can you help thinking?" Christian said: "I have to—it seems to me so awful that we might come to an end."

She closed her book, and it slipped off her lap. She went on: "There must be a future life, we're so incomplete. What's the good of your work, for instance? What's the use of developing if you have to stop?"

"I don't know," answered Harz. "I don't much care. All I know is, I've got to work."

"But why?"

"For happiness—the real happiness is fighting—the rest is nothing. If you have finished a thing, does it ever satisfy you? You look forward to the next thing at once; to wait is wretched!"

Christian clasped her hands behind her neck; sunlight flickered through the leaves on to the bosom of her dress.

"Ah! Stay like that!" cried Harz.

She let her eyes rest on his face, swinging her foot a little.

"You work because you must; but that's not enough. Why do you feel you must? I want to know what's behind. When I was travelling with Aunt Constance the winter before last we often talked—I've heard her discuss it with her friends. She says we move in circles till we reach Nirvana. But last winter I found I couldn't talk to her; it seemed as if she never really meant anything. Then I started reading—Kant and Hegel—"

"Ah!" put in Harz, "if they would teach me to draw better, or to see a new colour in a flower, or an expression in a face, I would read them all."

Christian leaned forward: "It must be right to get as near truth as possible; every step gained is something. You believe in truth; truth is the same as beauty—that was what you said—you try to paint the truth, you always see the beauty. But how can we know truth, unless we know what is at the root of it?"

"I—think," murmured Greta, sotto voce, "you see one way—and he sees another—because—you are not one person."

"Of course!" said Christian impatiently, "but why—"

A sound of humming interrupted her.

Nicholas Treffry was coming from the house, holding the Times in one hand, and a huge meerschaum pipe in the other.

"Aha!" he said to Harz: "how goes the picture?" and he lowered himself into a chair.

"Better to-day, Uncle?" said Christian softly.

Mr. Treffry growled. "Confounded humbugs, doctors!" he said. "Your father used to swear by them; why, his doctor killed him—made him drink such a lot of stuff!"

"Why then do you have a doctor, Uncle Nic?" asked Greta.

Mr. Treffry looked at her; his eyes twinkled. "I don't know, my dear. If they get half a chance, they won't let go of you!"

There had been a gentle breeze all day, but now it had died away; not a leaf quivered, not a blade of grass was stirring; from the house were heard faint sounds as of some one playing on a pipe. A blackbird came hopping down the path.

"When you were a boy, did you go after birds' nests, Uncle Nic?" Greta whispered.

"I believe you, Greta." The blackbird hopped into the shrubbery.

"You frightened him, Uncle Nic! Papa says that at Schloss Konig, where he lived when he was young, he would always be after jackdaws' nests."

"Gammon, Greta. Your father never took a jackdaw's nest, his legs are much too round!"

"Are you fond of birds, Uncle Nic?"

"Ask me another, Greta! Well, I s'pose so."

"Then why did you go bird-nesting? I think it is cruel"

Mr. Treffry coughed behind his paper: "There you have me, Greta," he remarked.

Harz began to gather his brushes: "Thank you," he said, "that's all I can do to-day."

"Can I look?" Mr. Treffry inquired.

"Certainly!"

Uncle Nic got up slowly, and stood in front of the picture. "When it's for sale," he said at last, "I'll buy it."

Harz bowed; but for some reason he felt annoyed, as if he had been asked to part with something personal.

"I thank you," he said. A gong sounded.

"You'll stay and have a snack with us?" said Mr. Treffry; "the doctor's stopping." Gathering up his paper, he moved off to the house with his hand on Greta's shoulder, the terrier running in front. Harz and Christian were left alone. He was scraping his palette, and she was sitting with her elbows resting on her knees; between them, a gleam of sunlight dyed the path golden. It was evening already; the bushes and the flowers, after the day's heat, were breathing out perfume; the birds had started their evensong.

"Are you tired of sitting for your portrait, Fraulein Christian?"

Christian shook her head.

"I shall get something into it that everybody does not see—something behind the surface, that will last."

Christian said slowly: "That's like a challenge. You were right when you said fighting is happiness—for yourself, but not for me. I'm a coward. I hate to hurt people, I like them to like me. If you had to do anything that would make them hate you, you would do it all the same, if it helped your work; that's fine—it's what I can't do. It's—it's everything. Do you like Uncle Nic?"

The young painter looked towards the house, where under the veranda old Nicholas Treffry was still in sight; a smile came on his lips.

"If I were the finest painter in the world, he wouldn't think anything of me for it, I'm afraid; but if I could show him handfuls of big cheques for bad pictures I had painted, he would respect me."

She smiled, and said: "I love him."

"Then I shall like him," Harz answered simply.

She put her hand out, and her fingers met his. "We shall be late," she said, glowing, and catching up her book: "I'm always late!"

VII

There was one other guest at dinner, a well-groomed person with pale, fattish face, dark eyes, and hair thin on the temples, whose clothes had a military cut. He looked like a man fond of ease, who had gone out of his groove, and collided with life. Herr Paul introduced him as Count Mario Sarelli.

Two hanging lamps with crimson shades threw a rosy light over the table, where, in the centre stood a silver basket, full of irises. Through the open windows the garden was all clusters of black foliage in the dying light. Moths fluttered round the lamps; Greta, following them with her eyes, gave quite audible sighs of pleasure when they escaped. Both girls wore white, and Harz, who sat opposite Christian, kept looking at her, and wondering why he had not painted her in that dress.

Mrs. Decie understood the art of dining—the dinner, ordered by Herr Paul, was admirable; the servants silent as their shadows; there was always a hum of conversation.

Sarelli, who sat on her right hand, seemed to partake of little except olives, which he dipped into a glass of sherry. He turned his black, solemn eyes silently from face to face, now and then asking the meaning of an English word. After a discussion on modern Rome, it was debated whether or no a criminal could be told by the expression of his face.

"Crime," said Mrs. Decie, passing her hand across her brow—"crime is but the hallmark of strong individuality."

Miss Naylor, gushing rather pink, stammered: "A great crime must show itself—a murder. Why, of course!"

"If that were so," said Dawney, "we should only have to look about us—no more detectives."

Miss Naylor rejoined with slight severity: "I cannot conceive that such a thing can pass the human face by, leaving no impression!"

Harz said abruptly: "There are worse things than murder."

"Ah! par exemple!" said Sarelli.

There was a slight stir all round the table.

"Verry good," cried out Herr Paul, "a vot' sante, cher."

Miss Naylor shivered, as if some one had put a penny down her back; and Mrs. Decie, leaning towards Harz, smiled like one who has made a pet dog do a trick. Christian alone was motionless, looking thoughtfully at Harz.

"I saw a man tried for murder once," he said, "a murder for revenge; I watched the judge, and I thought all the time: 'I'd rather be that murderer than you; I've never seen a meaner face; you crawl through life; you're not a criminal, simply because you haven't the courage.'"

In the dubious silence following the painter's speech, Mr. Treffry could distinctly be heard humming. Then Sarelli said: "What do you say to anarchists, who are not men, but savage beasts, whom I would tear to pieces!"

"As to that," Harz answered defiantly, "it maybe wise to hang them, but then there are so many other men that it would be wise to hang."

"How can we tell what they went through; what their lives were?" murmured Christian.

Miss Naylor, who had been rolling a pellet of bread, concealed it hastily. "They are—always given a chance to—repent—I believe," she said.

"For what they are about to receive," drawled Dawney.

Mrs. Decie signalled with her fan: "We are trying to express the inexpressible—shall we go into the garden?"

All rose; Harz stood by the window, and in passing, Christian looked at him.

He sat down again with a sudden sense of loss. There was no white figure opposite now. Raising his eyes he met Sarelli's. The Italian was regarding him with a curious stare.

Herr Paul began retailing apiece of scandal he had heard that afternoon.

"Shocking affair!" he said; "I could never have believed it of her! B—-is quite beside himself. Yesterday there was a row, it seems!"

"There has been one every day for months," muttered Dawney.

"But to leave without a word, and go no one knows where! B—-is 'viveur' no doubt, mais, mon Dieu, que voulez vous? She was always a poor, pale thing. Why! when my—-" he flourished his cigar; "I was not always—what I should have been—one lives in a world of flesh and blood—-we are not all angels—-que diable! But this is a very vulgar business. She goes off; leaves everything—-without a word; and B—-is very fond of her. These things are not done!" the starched bosom of his shirt seemed swollen by indignation.

Mr. Treffry, with a heavy hand on the table, eyed him sideways. Dawney said slowly:

"B—-is a beast; I'm sorry for the poor woman; but what can she do alone?"

"There is, no doubt, a man," put in Sarelli.

Herr Paul muttered: "Who knows?"

"What is B—-going to do?" said Dawney.

"Ah!" said Herr Paul. "He is fond of her. He is a chap of resolution, he will get her back. He told me: 'Well, you know, I shall follow her wherever she goes till she comes back.' He will do it, he is a determined chap; he will follow her wherever she goes."

Mr. Treffry drank his wine off at a gulp, and sucked his moustache in sharply.

"She was a fool to marry him," said Dawney; "they haven't a point in common; she hates him like poison, and she's the better of the two. But it doesn't pay a woman to run off like that. B—-had better hurry up, though. What do you think, sir?" he said to Mr. Treffry.

"Eh?" said Mr. Treffry; "how should I know? Ask Paul there, he's one of your moral men, or Count Sarelli."

The latter said impassively: "If I cared for her I should very likely kill her—if not—" he shrugged his shoulders.

Harz, who was watching, was reminded of his other words at dinner, "wild beasts whom I would tear to pieces." He looked with interest at this quiet man who said these extremely ferocious things, and thought: 'I should like to paint that fellow.'

Herr Paul twirled his wine-glass in his fingers. "There are family ties," he said, "there is society, there is decency; a wife should be with her husband. B—-will do quite right. He must go after her; she will not perhaps come back at first; he will follow her; she will begin to think, 'I am helpless—I am ridiculous!' A woman is soon beaten. They will return. She is once more with her husband—Society will forgive, it will be all right."

"By Jove, Paul," growled Mr. Treffry, "wonderful power of argument!"

"A wife is a wife," pursued Herr Paul; "a man has a right to her society."

"What do you say to that, sir?" asked Dawney.

Mr. Treffry tugged at his beard: "Make a woman live with you, if she don't want to? I call it low."

"But, my dear," exclaimed Herr Paul, "how should you know? You have not been married."

"No, thank the Lord!" Mr. Treffry replied.

"But looking at the question broadly, sir," said Dawney; "if a husband always lets his wife do as she likes, how would the thing work out? What becomes of the marriage tie?"

"The marriage tie," growled Mr. Treffry, "is the biggest thing there is! But, by Jove, Doctor, I'm a Dutchman if hunting women ever helped the marriage tie!"

"I am not thinking of myself," Herr Paul cried out, "I think of the community. There are rights."

"A decent community never yet asked a man to tread on his self-respect. If I get my fingers skinned over my marriage, which I undertake at my own risk, what's the community to do with it? D'you think I'm going to whine to it to put the plaster on? As to rights, it'd be a deuced sight better for us all if there wasn't such a fuss about 'em. Leave that to women! I don't give a tinker's damn for men who talk about their rights in such matters."

Sarelli rose. "But your honour," he said, "there is your honour!"

Mr. Treffry stared at him.

"Honour! If huntin' women's your idea of honour, well—it isn't mine."

"Then you'd forgive her, sir, whatever happened," Dawney said.

"Forgiveness is another thing. I leave that to your sanctimonious beggars. But, hunt a woman! Hang it, sir, I'm not a cad!" and bringing his hand down with a rattle, he added: "This is a subject that don't bear talking of."

Sarelli fell back in his seat, twirling his moustaches fiercely. Harz, who had risen, looked at Christian's empty place.

'If I were married!' he thought suddenly.

Herr Paul, with a somewhat vinous glare, still muttered, "But your duty to the family!"

Harz slipped through the window. The moon was like a wonderful white lantern in the purple sky; there was but a smoulder of stars. Beneath the softness of the air was the iciness of the snow; it made him want to run and leap. A sleepy beetle dropped on its back; he turned it over and watched it scurry across the grass.

Someone was playing Schumann's Kinderscenen. Harz stood still to listen. The notes came twining, weaving round his thoughts; the whole night seemed full of girlish voices, of hopes and fancies, soaring away to mountain heights—invisible, yet present. Between the stems of the acacia-trees he could see the flicker of white dresses, where Christian and Greta were walking arm in arm. He went towards them; the blood flushed up in his face, he felt almost surfeited by some sweet emotion. Then, in sudden horror, he stood still. He was in love! With nothing done with everything before him! He was going to bow down to a face! The flicker of the dresses was no longer visible. He would not be fettered, he would stamp it out! He turned away; but with each step, something seemed to jab at his heart.

Round the corner of the house, in the shadow of the wall, Dominique, the Luganese, in embroidered slippers, was smoking a long cherry-wood pipe, leaning against a tree—Mephistopheles in evening clothes. Harz went up to him.

"Lend me a pencil, Dominique."

"Bien, M'sieu."

Resting a card against the tree Harz wrote to Mrs. Decie: "Forgive me, I am obliged to go away. In a few days I shall hope to return, and finish the picture of your nieces."

He sent Dominique for his hat. During the man's absence he was on the point of tearing up the card and going back into the house.

When the Luganese returned he thrust the card into his hand, and walked out between the tall poplars, waiting, like ragged ghosts, silver with moonlight.

VIII

Harz walked away along the road. A dog was howling. The sound seemed too appropriate. He put his fingers to his ears, but the lugubrious noise passed those barriers, and made its way into his heart. Was there nothing that would put an end to this emotion? It was no better in the old house on the wall; he spent the night tramping up and down.

Just before daybreak he slipped out with a knapsack, taking the road towards Meran.

He had not quite passed through Gries when he overtook a man walking in the middle of the road and leaving a trail of cigar smoke behind him.

"Ah! my friend," the smoker said, "you walk early; are you going my way?"

It was Count Sarelli. The raw light had imparted a grey tinge to his pale face, the growth of his beard showed black already beneath the skin; his thumbs were hooked in the pockets of a closely buttoned coat, he gesticulated with his fingers.

"You are making a journey?" he said, nodding at the knapsack. "You are early—I am late; our friend has admirable kummel—I have drunk too much. You have not been to bed, I think? If there is no sleep in one's bed it is no good going to look for it. You find that? It is better to drink kummel...! Pardon! You are doing the right thing: get away! Get away as fast as possible! Don't wait, and let it catch you!"

Harz stared at him amazed.

"Pardon!" Sarelli said again, raising his hat, "that girl—the white girl—I saw. You do well to get away!" he swayed a little as he walked. "That old fellow—what is his name-Trrreffr-ry! What ideas of honour!" He mumbled: "Honour is an abstraction! If a man is not true to an abstraction, he is a low type; but wait a minute!"

He put his hand to his side as though in pain.

The hedges were brightening with a faint pinky glow; there was no sound on the long, deserted road, but that of their footsteps; suddenly a bird commenced to chirp, another answered—the world seemed full of these little voices.

Sarelli stopped.

"That white girl," he said, speaking with rapidity. "Yes! You do well! get away! Don't let it catch you! I waited, it caught me—what happened? Everything horrible—and now—kummel!" Laughing a thick laugh, he gave a twirl to his moustache, and swaggered on.

"I was a fine fellow—nothing too big for Mario Sarelli; the regiment looked to me. Then she came— with her eyes and her white dress, always white, like this one; the little mole on her chin, her hands for ever moving—their touch as warm as sunbeams. Then, no longer Sarelli this, and that! The little house close to the ramparts! Two arms, two eyes, and nothing here," he tapped his breast, "but flames that made ashes quickly—in her, like this ash—!" he flicked the white flake off his cigar. "It's droll! You agree, hein? Some day I shall go back and kill her. In the meantime—kummel!"

He stopped at a house close to the road, and stood still, his teeth bared in a grin.

"But I bore you," he said. His cigar, flung down, sputtered forth its sparks on the road in front of Harz. "I live here—good-morning! You are a man for work—your honour is your Art! I know, and you are young! The man who loves flesh better than his honour is a low type—I am a low type. I! Mario Sarelli, a low type! I love flesh better than my honour!"

He remained swaying at the gate with the grin fixed on his face; then staggered up the steps, and banged the door. But before Harz had walked on, he again appeared, beckoning, in the doorway. Obeying an impulse, Harz went in.

"We will make a night of it," said Sarelli; "wine, brandy, kummel? I am virtuous—kummel it must be for me!"

He sat down at a piano, and began to touch the keys. Harz poured out some wine. Sarelli nodded.

"You begin with that? Allegro—piu—presto!

"Wine—brandy—kummel!" he quickened the time of the tune: "it is not too long a passage, and this"—he took his hands off the keys—"comes after."

Harz smiled.

"Some men do not kill themselves," he said.

Sarelli, who was bending and swaying to the music of a tarantella, broke off, and letting his eyes rest on the painter, began playing Schumann's Kinderscenen. Harz leaped to his feet.

"Stop that!" he cried.

"It pricks you?" said Sarelli suavely; "what do you think of this?" he played again, crouching over the piano, and making the notes sound like the crying of a wounded animal.

"For me!" he said, swinging round, and rising.

"Your health! And so you don't believe in suicide, but in murder? The custom is the other way; but you don't believe in customs? Customs are only for Society?" He drank a glass of kummel. "You do not love Society?"

Harz looked at him intently; he did not want to quarrel.

"I am not too fond of other people's thoughts," he said at last; "I prefer to think my own."

"And is Society never right? That poor Society!"

"Society! What is Society—a few men in good coats? What has it done for me?"

Sarelli bit the end off a cigar.

"Ah!" he said; "now we are coming to it. It is good to be an artist, a fine bantam of an artist; where other men have their dis-ci-pline, he has his, what shall we say—his mound of roses?"

The painter started to his feet.

"Yes," said Sarelli, with a hiccough, "you are a fine fellow!"

"And you are drunk!" cried Harz.

"A little drunk—not much, not enough to matter!"

Harz broke into laughter. It was crazy to stay there listening to this mad fellow. What had brought him in? He moved towards the door.

"Ah!" said Sarelli, "but it is no good going to bed—let us talk. I have a lot to say—it is pleasant to talk to anarchists at times."

Full daylight was already coming through the chinks of the shutters.

"You are all anarchists, you painters, you writing fellows. You live by playing ball with facts. Images— nothing solid—hein? You're all for new things too, to tickle your nerves. No discipline! True anarchists, every one of you!"

Harz poured out another glass of wine and drank it off. The man's feverish excitement was catching.

"Only fools," he replied, "take things for granted. As for discipline, what do you aristocrats, or bourgeois know of discipline? Have you ever been hungry? Have you ever had your soul down on its back?"

"Soul on its back? That is good!"

"A man's no use," cried Harz, "if he's always thinking of what others think; he must stand on his own legs."

"He must not then consider other people?"

"Not from cowardice anyway."

Sarelli drank.

"What would you do," he said, striking his chest, "if you had a devil-here? Would you go to bed?"

A sort of pity seized on Harz. He wanted to say something that would be consoling but could find no words; and suddenly he felt disgusted. What link was there between him and this man; between his love and this man's love?

"Harz!" muttered Sarelli; "Harz means 'tar,' hein? Your family is not an old one?"

Harz glared, and said: "My father is a peasant."

Sarelli lifted the kummel bottle and emptied it into his glass, with a steady hand.

"You're honest—and we both have devils. I forgot; I brought you in to see a picture!"

He threw wide the shutters; the windows were already open, and a rush of air came in.

"Ah!" he said, sniffing, "smells of the earth, nicht wahr, Herr Artist? You should know—it belongs to your father.... Come, here's my picture; a Correggio! What do you think of it?"

"It is a copy."

"You think?"

"I know."

"Then you have given me the lie, Signor," and drawing out his handkerchief Sarelli flicked it in the painter's face.

Harz turned white.

"Duelling is a good custom!" said Sarelli. "I shall have the honour to teach you just this one, unless you are afraid. Here are pistols—this room is twenty feet across at least, twenty feet is no bad distance."

And pulling out a drawer he took two pistols from a case, and put them on the table.

"The light is good—but perhaps you are afraid."

"Give me one!" shouted the infuriated painter; "and go to the devil for a fool."

"One moment!" Sarelli murmured: "I will load them, they are more useful loaded."

Harz leaned out of the window; his head was in a whirl. 'What on earth is happening?' he thought. 'He's mad—or I am! Confound him! I'm not going to be killed!' He turned and went towards the table. Sarelli's head was sunk on his arms, he was asleep. Harz methodically took up the pistols, and put them back into the drawer. A sound made him turn his head; there stood a tall, strong young woman in a loose gown caught together on her chest. Her grey eyes glanced from the painter to the bottles, from the bottles to the pistol-case. A simple reasoning, which struck Harz as comic.

"It is often like this," she said in the country patois; "der Herr must not be frightened."

Lifting the motionless Sarelli as if he were a baby, she laid him on a couch.

"Ah!" she said, sitting down and resting her elbow on the table; "he will not wake!"

Harz bowed to her; her patient figure, in spite of its youth and strength, seemed to him pathetic. Taking up his knapsack, he went out.

The smoke of cottages rose straight; wisps of mist were wandering about the valley, and the songs of birds dropping like blessings. All over the grass the spiders had spun a sea of threads that bent and quivered to the pressure of the air, like fairy tight-ropes.

All that day he tramped.

Blacksmiths, tall stout men with knotted muscles, sleepy eyes, and great fair beards, came out of their forges to stretch and wipe their brows, and stare at him.

Teams of white oxen, waiting to be harnessed, lashed their tails against their flanks, moving their heads slowly from side to side in the heat. Old women at chalet doors blinked and knitted.

The white houses, with gaping caves of storage under the roofs, the red church spire, the clinking of hammers in the forges, the slow stamping of oxen-all spoke of sleepy toil, without ideas or ambition. Harz knew it all too well; like the earth's odour, it belonged to him, as Sarelli had said.

Towards sunset coming to a copse of larches, he sat down to rest. It was very still, but for the tinkle of cowbells, and, from somewhere in the distance, the sound of dropping logs.

Two barefooted little boys came from the wood, marching earnestly along, and looking at Harz as if he were a monster. Once past him, they began to run.

'At their age,' he thought, 'I should have done the same.' A hundred memories rushed into his mind.

He looked down at the village straggling below—white houses with russet tiles and crowns of smoke, vineyards where the young leaves were beginning to unfold, the red-capped spire, a thread of bubbling stream, an old stone cross. He had been fourteen years struggling up from all this; and now just as he had breathing space, and the time to give himself wholly to his work—this weakness was upon him! Better, a thousand times, to give her up!

In a house or two lights began to wink; the scent of wood smoke reached him, the distant chimes of bells, the burring of a stream.

IX

Next day his one thought was to get back to work. He arrived at the studio in the afternoon, and, laying in provisions, barricaded the lower door. For three days he did not go out; on the fourth day he went to Villa Rubein....

Schloss Runkelstein—grey, blind, strengthless—still keeps the valley. The windows which once, like eyes, watched men and horses creeping through the snow, braved the splutter of guns and the gleam of torches, are now holes for the birds to nest in. Tangled creepers have spread to the very summits of the walls. In the keep, instead of grim men in armour, there is a wooden board recording the history of the castle and instructing visitors on the subject of refreshments. Only at night, when the cold moon blanches everything, the castle stands like the grim ghost of its old self, high above the river.

After a long morning's sitting the girls had started forth with Harz and Dawney to spend the afternoon at the ruin; Miss Naylor, kept at home by headache, watched them depart with words of caution against sunstroke, stinging nettles, and strange dogs.

Since the painter's return Christian and he had hardly spoken to each other. Below the battlement on which they sat, in a railed gallery with little tables, Dawney and Greta were playing dominoes, two soldiers drinking beer, and at the top of a flight of stairs the Custodian's wife sewing at a garment. Christian said suddenly: "I thought we were friends."

"Well, Fraulein Christian, aren't we?"

"You went away without a word; friends don't do that."

Harz bit his lips.

"I don't think you care," she went on with a sort of desperate haste, "whether you hurt people or not. You have been here all this time without even going to see your father and mother."

"Do you think they would want to see me?"

Christian looked up.

"It's all been so soft for you," he said bitterly; "you don't understand."

He turned his head away, and then burst out: "I'm proud to come straight from the soil—I wouldn't have it otherwise; but they are of 'the people,' everything is narrow with them—they only understand what they can see and touch."

"I'm sorry I spoke like that," said Christian softly; "you've never told me about yourself."

There was something just a little cruel in the way the painter looked at her, then seeming to feel compunction, he said quickly: "I always hated—the peasant life—I wanted to get away into the world; I had a feeling in here—I wanted—I don't know what I wanted! I did run away at last to a house-painter at Meran. The priest wrote me a letter from my father—they threw me off; that's all."

Christian's eyes were very bright, her lips moved, like the lips of a child listening to a story.

"Go on," she said.

"I stayed at Meran two years, till I'd learnt all I could there, then a brother of my mother's helped me to get to Vienna; I was lucky enough to find work with a man who used to decorate churches. We went about the country together. Once when he was ill I painted the roof of a church entirely by myself; I lay on my back on the scaffold boards all day for a week—I was proud of that roof." He paused.

"When did you begin painting pictures?"

"A friend asked me why I didn't try for the Academie. That started me going to the night schools; I worked every minute—I had to get my living as well, of course, so I worked at night.

"Then when the examination came, I thought I could do nothing—it was just as if I had never had a brush or pencil in my hand. But the second day a professor in passing me said, 'Good! Quite good!' That gave me courage. I was sure I had failed though; but I was second out of sixty."

Christian nodded.

"To work in the schools after that I had to give up my business, of course. There was only one teacher who ever taught me anything; the others all seemed fools. This man would come and rub out what you'd done with his sleeve. I used to cry with rage—but I told him I could only learn from him, and he was so astonished that he got me into his class."

"But how did you live without money?" asked Christian.

His face burned with a dark flush. "I don't know how I lived; you must have been through these things to know, you would never understand."

"But I want to understand, please."

"What do you want me to tell you? How I went twice a week to eat free dinners! How I took charity! How I was hungry! There was a rich cousin of my mother's—I used to go to him. I didn't like it. But if you're starving in the winter."

Christian put out her hand.

"I used to borrow apronsful of coals from other students who were as poor—but I never went to the rich students."

The flush had died out of his face.

"That sort of thing makes you hate the world! You work till you stagger; you're cold and hungry; you see rich people in their carriages, wrapped in furs, and all the time you want to do something great. You pray for a chance, any chance; nothing comes to the poor! It makes you hate the world."

Christian's eyes filled with tears. He went on:

"But I wasn't the only one in that condition; we used to meet. Garin, a Russian with a brown beard and patches of cheek showing through, and yellow teeth, who always looked hungry. Paunitz, who came from sympathy! He had fat cheeks and little eyes, and a big gold chain—the swine! And little Misek. It was in his room we met, with the paper peeling off the walls, and two doors with cracks in them, so that there was always a draught. We used to sit on his bed, and pull the dirty blankets over us for warmth; and smoke—tobacco was the last thing we ever went without. Over the bed was a Virgin and Child—Misek was a very devout Catholic; but one day when he had had no dinner and a dealer had kept his picture without paying him, he took the image and threw it on the floor before our eyes; it broke, and he trampled on the bits. Lendorf was another, a heavy fellow who was always puffing out his white cheeks and smiting himself, and saying: 'Cursed society!' And Schonborn, an aristocrat who had quarrelled with his family. He was the poorest of us all; but only he and I would ever have dared to do anything—they all knew that!"

Christian listened with awe. "Do you mean?" she said, "do you mean, that you—?"

"You see! you're afraid of me at once. It's impossible even for you to understand. It only makes you afraid. A hungry man living on charity, sick with rage and shame, is a wolf even to you!"

Christian looked straight into his eyes.

"That's not true. If I can't understand, I can feel. Would you be the same now if it were to come again?"

"Yes, it drives me mad even now to think of people fatted with prosperity, sneering and holding up their hands at poor devils who have suffered ten times more than the most those soft animals could bear. I'm older; I've lived—I know things can't be put right by violence—nothing will put things right, but that doesn't stop my feeling."

"Did you do anything? You must tell me all now."

"We talked—we were always talking."

"No, tell me everything!"

Unconsciously she claimed, and he seemed unconsciously to admit her right to this knowledge.

"There's not much to tell. One day we began talking in low voices—Garin began it; he had been in some affair in Russia. We took an oath; after that we never raised our voices. We had a plan. It was all new to me, and I hated the whole thing—but I was always hungry, or sick from taking charity, and I would have done anything. They knew that; they used to look at me and Schonborn; we knew that no one else had any courage. He and I were great friends, but we never talked of that; we tried to keep our minds away from the thought of it. If we had a good day and were not so hungry, it seemed unnatural; but when the day had not been good—then it seemed natural enough. I wasn't afraid, but I used to wake up in the night; I hated the oath we had taken, I hated every one of those fellows; the thing was not what I was made for, it wasn't my work, it wasn't my nature, it was forced on me—I hated it, but sometimes I was like a madman."

"Yes, yes," she murmured.

"All this time I was working at the Academie, and learning all I could.... One evening that we met, Paunitz was not there. Misek was telling us how the thing had been arranged. Schonborn and I looked at each other—it was warm—perhaps we were not hungry—it was springtime, too, and in the Spring it's different. There is something."

Christian nodded.

"While we were talking there came a knock at the door. Lendorf put his eye to the keyhole, and made a sign. The police were there. Nobody said anything, but Misek crawled under the bed; we all followed; and the knocking grew louder and louder. In the wall at the back of the bed was a little door into an empty cellar. We crept through. There was a trap-door behind some cases, where they used to roll barrels in. We crawled through that into the back street. We went different ways."

He paused, and Christian gasped.

"I thought I would get my money, but there was a policeman before my door. They had us finely. It was Paunitz; if I met him even now I should wring his neck. I swore I wouldn't be caught, but I had no idea where to go. Then I thought of a little Italian barber who used to shave me when I had money for a shave; I knew he would help. He belonged to some Italian Society; he often talked to me, under his breath, of course. I went to him. He was shaving himself before going to a ball. I told him what had happened; it was funny to see him put his back against the door. He was very frightened, understanding this sort of thing better than I did—for I was only twenty then. He shaved my head and moustache and put me on a fair wig. Then he brought me macaroni, and some meat, to eat. He gave me a big fair moustache, and a cap, and hid the moustache in the lining. He brought me a cloak of his own, and four gulden. All the time he was extremely frightened, and kept listening, and saying: 'Eat!'

"When I had done, he just said: 'Go away, I refuse to know anything more of you.'

"I thanked him and went out. I walked about all that night; for I couldn't think of anything to do or anywhere to go. In the morning I slept on a seat in one of the squares. Then I thought I would go to the Gallerien; and I spent the whole day looking at the pictures. When the Galleries were shut I was very tired, so I went into a cafe, and had some beer. When I came out I sat on the same seat in the Square. I meant to wait till dark and then walk out of the city and take the train at some little station, but while I was sitting there I went to sleep. A policeman woke me. He had my wig in his hand.

"'Why do you wear a wig?' he said.

"I answered: 'Because I am bald.'

"'No,' he said, 'you're not bald, you've been shaved. I can feel the hair coming.'

"He put his finger on my head. I felt reckless and laughed.

"'Ah!' he said, 'you'll come with me and explain all this; your nose and eyes are looked for.'

"I went with him quietly to the police-station...."

Harz seemed carried away by his story. His quick dark face worked, his steel-grey eyes stared as though he were again passing through all these long-past emotions.

The hot sun struck down; Christian drew herself together, sitting with her hands clasped round her knees.

X

"I didn't care by then what came of it. I didn't even think what I was going to say. He led me down a passage to a room with bars across the windows and long seats, and maps on the walls. We sat and waited. He kept his eye on me all the time; and I saw no hope. Presently the Inspector came. 'Bring him in here,' he said; I remember feeling I could kill him for ordering me about! We went into the next room. It had a large clock, a writing-table, and a window, without bars, looking on a courtyard. Long policemen's coats and caps were hanging from some pegs. The Inspector told me to take off my cap. I took it off, wig and all. He asked me who I was, but I refused to answer. Just then there was a loud sound of voices in the room we had come from. The Inspector told the policeman to look after me, and went to see what it was. I could hear him talking. He called out: 'Come here, Becker!' I stood very quiet, and Becker went towards the door. I heard the Inspector say: 'Go and find Schwartz, I will see after this fellow.' The policeman went, and the Inspector stood with his back to me in the half-open door, and began again to talk to the man in the other room. Once or twice he looked round at me, but I stood quiet all the time. They began to disagree, and their voices got angry. The Inspector moved a little into the other room. 'Now!' I thought, and slipped off my cloak. I hooked off a policeman's coat and cap, and put them on. My heart beat till I felt sick. I went on tiptoe to the window. There was no one outside, but at the entrance a man was holding some horses. I opened the window a little and held my breath. I heard the Inspector say: 'I will report you for impertinence!' and slipped through the window. The coat came down nearly to my heels, and the cap over my eyes. I walked up to the man with the horses, and said: 'Good-evening.' One of the horses had begun to kick, and he only grunted at me. I got into a passing tram; it was five minutes to the West Bahnhof; I got out there. There was a train starting; they were shouting 'Einsteigen!' I ran. The collector tried to stop me. I shouted: 'Business—important!' He let me by. I jumped into a carriage. The train started."

He paused, and Christian heaved a sigh.

Harz went on, twisting a twig of ivy in his hands: "There was another man in the carriage reading a paper. Presently I said to him, 'Where do we stop first?' 'St. Polten.' Then I knew it was the Munich express—St. Polten, Amstetten, Linz, and Salzburg—four stops before the frontier. The man put down his paper and looked at me; he had a big fair moustache and rather shabby clothes. His looking at me disturbed me, for I thought every minute he would say: 'You're no policeman!' And suddenly it came into my mind that if they looked for me in this train, it would be as a policeman!— they would know, of course, at the station that a policeman had run past at the last minute. I wanted to get rid of the coat and cap, but the man was there, and I didn't like to move out of the carriage for other people to notice. So I sat on. We came to St. Polten at last. The man in my carriage took his bag, got out, and left his paper on the seat. We started again; I breathed at last, and as soon as I could took the cap and coat and threw them out into the darkness. I thought: 'I shall get across the frontier now.' I took my own cap out and found the moustache Luigi gave me; rubbed my clothes as clean as possible; stuck on the moustache, and with some little ends of chalk in my pocket made my eyebrows light; then drew some lines in my face to make it older, and pulled my cap well down above my wig. I did it pretty well—I was quite like the man who had got out. I sat in his corner, took up his newspaper, and waited for Amstetten. It seemed a tremendous time before we got there. From behind my paper I could see five or six policemen on the platform, one quite close. He opened the door, looked at me, and walked through the carriage into the corridor. I took some tobacco and rolled up a cigarette, but it shook, Harz lifted the ivy twig, like this. In a minute the conductor and two more policemen came. 'He was here,' said the conductor, 'with this gentleman.' One of them looked at me, and asked: 'Have you seen a policeman travelling on this train?' 'Yes,' I said. 'Where?' 'He got out at St. Polten.' The policeman asked the conductor: 'Did you see him get out there?' The conductor shook his head. I said: 'He got out as the train was moving.' 'Ah!' said the policeman, 'what was he like?' 'Rather short, and no moustache. Why?' 'Did you notice anything unusual?' 'No,' I said, 'only that he wore coloured trousers. What's the matter?' One policeman said to the other: 'That's our man! Send a telegram to St. Polten; he has more than an hour's start.' He asked me where I was going. I told him: 'Linz.' 'Ah!' he said, 'you'll have to give evidence; your name and address please?' 'Josef Reinhardt, 17 Donau Strasse.' He wrote it down. The conductor said: 'We are late, can we start?' They shut the door. I heard them say to the conductor: 'Search again at Linz, and report to the Inspector there.' They hurried on to the platform, and we started. At first I thought I would get out as soon as the train had left the station. Then, that I should be too far from the frontier; better to go on to Linz and take my chance there. I sat still and tried not to think.

"After a long time, we began to run more slowly. I put my head out and could see in the distance a ring of lights hanging in the blackness. I loosened the carriage door and waited for the train to run slower still; I didn't mean to go into Linz like a rat into a trap. At last I could wait no longer; I opened the door, jumped and fell into some bushes. I was not much hurt, but bruised, and the breath knocked out of me. As soon as I could, I crawled out. It was very dark. I felt heavy and sore, and for some time went stumbling in and out amongst trees. Presently I came to a clear space; on one side I could see the town's shape drawn in lighted lamps, and on the other a dark mass, which I think was forest; in the distance too was a thin chain of lights. I thought: 'They must be the lights of a bridge.' Just then the moon came out, and I could see the river shining below. It was cold and damp, and I walked quickly. At last I came out on a road, past houses and barking dogs, down to the river bank; there I sat against a shed and went to sleep. I woke very stiff. It was darker than before; the moon was gone. I could just see the river. I stumbled on, to get through the town before dawn. It was all black shapes-houses and sheds, and the smell of the river, the smell of rotting hay, apples, tar, mud, fish; and here and there on a wharf a lantern. I stumbled over casks and ropes and boxes; I saw I should never get clear—the dawn had begun already on the other side. Some men came from a house behind me. I bent, and crept behind some barrels. They passed along the wharf; they seemed to drop into the river. I heard one of them say: 'Passau before night.' I stood up and saw they had walked on board a steamer which was lying head up-stream, with some barges in tow. There was a plank laid to the steamer, and a lantern at the other end. I could hear the fellows moving below deck, getting up steam. I ran across the plank and crept to the end of the steamer. I meant to go with them to Passau! The rope which towed the barges was nearly taut; and I knew if I could get on to the barges I should be safe. I climbed down on this rope and crawled along. I was desperate, I knew they'd soon be coming up, and it was getting light. I thought I should fall into the water several times, but I got to the barge at last. It was laden with straw. There was nobody on board. I was hungry and thirsty—I looked for something to eat; there was nothing but the ashes of a fire and a man's coat. I crept into the straw. Soon a boat brought men, one for each barge, and there were sounds of steam. As soon as we began moving through the water, I fell asleep. When I woke we were creeping through a heavy mist. I made a little hole in the straw and saw the bargeman. He was sitting by a fire at the barge's edge, so that the sparks and smoke blew away over the water. He ate and drank with both hands, and funny enough he looked in the mist, like a big bird flapping its wings; there was a good smell of coffee, and I sneezed. How the fellow started! But presently he took a pitchfork and prodded the straw. Then I stood up. I couldn't help laughing, he was so surprised—a huge, dark man, with a great black beard. I pointed to the fire and said 'Give me some, brother!' He pulled me out of the straw; I was so stiff, I couldn't move. I sat by the fire, and ate black bread and turnips, and drank coffee; while he stood by, watching me and muttering. I couldn't understand him well—he spoke a dialect from Hungary. He asked me: How I got there—who I was—where I was from? I looked up in his face, and he looked down at me, sucking his pipe. He was a big man, he lived alone on the river, and I was tired of telling lies, so I told him the whole thing. When I had done he just grunted. I can see him now standing over me, with the mist hanging in his beard, and his great naked arms. He drew me some water, and I washed and showed him my wig and moustache, and threw them overboard. All that day we lay out on the barge in the mist, with our feet to the fire, smoking; now and then he would spit into the ashes and mutter into his beard. I shall never forget that day. The steamer was like a monster with fiery nostrils, and the other barges were dumb creatures with eyes, where the fires were; we couldn't see the bank, but now and then a bluff and high trees, or a castle, showed in the mist. If I had only had paint and canvas that day!" He sighed.

"It was early Spring, and the river was in flood; they were going to Regensburg to unload there, take fresh cargo, and back to Linz. As soon as the mist began to clear, the bargeman hid me in the straw. At Passau was the frontier; they lay there for the night, but nothing happened, and I slept in the straw. The next day I lay out on the barge deck; there was no mist, but I was free—the sun shone gold on the straw and the green sacking; the water seemed to dance, and I laughed—I laughed all the time, and the barge man laughed with me. A fine fellow he was! At Regensburg I helped them to unload; for more than a week we worked; they nicknamed me baldhead, and when it was all over I gave the money I earned for the unloading to the big bargeman. We kissed each other at parting. I had still three of the gulden that Luigi gave me, and I went to a house-painter and got work with him. For six months I stayed there to save money; then I wrote to my mother's cousin in Vienna, and told him I was going to London. He gave me an introduction to some friends there. I went to Hamburg, and from there to London in a cargo steamer, and I've never been back till now."

XI

After a minute's silence Christian said in a startled voice: "They could arrest you then!"

Harz laughed.

"If they knew; but it's seven years ago."

"Why did you come here, when it's so dangerous?"

"I had been working too hard, I wanted to see my country—after seven years, and when it's forbidden! But I'm ready to go back now." He looked down at her, frowning.

"Had you a hard time in London, too?"

"Harder, at first—I couldn't speak the language. In my profession it's hard work to get recognised, it's hard work to make a living. There are too many whose interest it is to keep you down—I shan't forget them."

"But every one is not like that?"

"No; there are fine fellows, too. I shan't forget them either. I can sell my pictures now; I'm no longer weak, and I promise you I shan't forget. If in the future I have power, and I shall have power—I shan't forget."

A shower of fine gravel came rattling on the wall. Dawney was standing below them with an amused expression on his upturned face.

"Are you going to stay there all night?" he asked. "Greta and I have bored each other."

"We're coming," called Christian hastily.

On the way back neither spoke a word, but when they reached the Villa, Harz took her hand, and said: "Fraulein Christian, I can't do any more with your picture. I shan't touch it again after this."

She made no answer, but they looked at each other, and both seemed to ask, to entreat, something more; then her eyes fell. He dropped her hand, and saying, "Good-night," ran after Dawney.

In the corridor, Dominique, carrying a dish of fruit, met the sisters; he informed them that Miss Naylor had retired to bed; that Herr Paul would not be home to dinner; his master was dining in his room; dinner would be served for Mrs. Decie and the two young ladies in a quarter of an hour: "And the fish is good to-night; little trouts! try them, Signorina!" He moved on quickly, softly, like a cat, the tails of his dress-coat flapping, and the heels of his white socks gleaming.

Christian ran upstairs. She flew about her room, feeling that if she once stood still it would all crystallise in hard painful thought, which motion alone kept away. She washed, changed her dress and shoes, and ran down to her uncle's room. Mr. Treffry had just finished dinner, pushed the little table back, and was sitting in his chair, with his glasses on his nose, reading the Tines. Christian touched his forehead with her lips.

"Glad to see you, Chris. Your stepfather's out to dinner, and I can't stand your aunt when she's in one of her talking moods—bit of a humbug, Chris, between ourselves; eh, isn't she?" His eyes twinkled.

Christian smiled. There was a curious happy restlessness in her that would not let her keep still.

"Picture finished?" Mr. Treffry asked suddenly, taking up the paper with a crackle. "Don't go and fall in love with the painter, Chris."

Christian was still enough now.

'Why not?' she thought. 'What should you know about him? Isn't he good enough for me?' A gong sounded.

"There's your dinner," Mr. Treffry remarked.

With sudden contrition she bent and kissed him.

But when she had left the room Mr. Treffry put down the Times and stared at the door, humming to himself, and thoughtfully fingering his chin.

Christian could not eat; she sat, indifferent to the hoverings of Dominique, tormented by uneasy fear and longings. She answered Mrs. Decie at random. Greta kept stealing looks at her from under her lashes.

"Decided characters are charming, don't you think so, Christian?" Mrs. Decie said, thrusting her chin a little forward, and modelling the words. "That is why I like Mr. Harz so much; such an immense advantage for a man to know his mind. You have only to look at that young man to see that he knows what he wants, and means to have it."

Christian pushed her plate away. Greta, flushing, said abruptly: "Doctor Edmund is not a decided character, I think. This afternoon he said: 'Shall I have some beer-yes, I shall—no, I shall not'; then he ordered the beer, so, when it came, he gave it to the soldiers."

Mrs. Decie turned her enigmatic smile from one girl to the other.

When dinner was over they went into her room. Greta stole at once to the piano, where her long hair fell almost to the keys; silently she sat there fingering the notes, smiling to herself, and looking at her aunt, who was reading Pater's essays. Christian too had taken up a book, but soon put it down—of several pages she had not understood a word. She went into the garden and wandered about the lawn, clasping her hands behind her head. The air was heavy; very distant thunder trembled among the mountains, flashes of summer lightning played over the trees; and two great moths were hovering about a rosebush. Christian watched their soft uncertain rushes. Going to the little summer-house she flung herself down on a seat, and pressed her hands to her heart.

There was a strange and sudden aching there. Was he going from her? If so, what would be left? How little and how narrow seemed the outlook of her life—with the world waiting for her, the world of beauty, effort, self-sacrifice, fidelity! It was as though a flash of that summer lightning had fled by, singeing her, taking from her all powers of flight, burning off her wings, as off one of those pale hovering moths. Tears started up, and trickled down her face. 'Blind!' she thought; 'how could I have been so blind?'

Some one came down the path.

"Who's there?" she cried.

Harz stood in the doorway.

"Why did you come out?" he said. "Ah! why did you come out?" He caught her hand; Christian tried to draw it from him, and to turn her eyes away, but she could not. He flung himself down on his knees, and cried: "I love you!"

In a rapture of soft terror Christian bent her forehead down to his hand.

"What are you doing?" she heard him say. "Is it possible that you love me?" and she felt his kisses on her hair.

"My sweet! it will be so hard for you; you are so little, so little, and so weak." Clasping his hand closer to her face, she murmured: "I don't care."

There was a long, soft silence, that seemed to last for ever. Suddenly she threw her arms round his neck and kissed him.

"Whatever comes!" she whispered, and gathering her dress, escaped from him into the darkness.

XII

Christian woke next morning with a smile. In her attitudes, her voice, her eyes, there was a happy and sweet seriousness, as if she were hugging some holy thought. After breakfast she took a book and sat in the open window, whence she could see the poplar-trees guarding the entrance. There was a breeze; the roses close by kept nodding to her; the cathedral bells were in full chime; bees hummed above the lavender; and in the sky soft clouds were floating like huge, white birds.

The sounds of Miss Naylor's staccato dictation travelled across the room, and Greta's sighs as she took it down, one eye on her paper, one eye on Scruff, who lay with a black ear flapped across his paw, and his tan eyebrows quivering. He was in disgrace, for Dominique, coming on him unawares, had seen him "say his prayers" before a pudding, and take the pudding for reward.

Christian put her book down gently, and slipped through the window. Harz was coming in from the road. "I am all yours!" she whispered. His fingers closed on hers, and he went into the house.

She slipped back, took up her book, and waited. It seemed long before he came out, but when he did he waved her back, and hurried on; she had a glimpse of his face, white to the lips. Feeling faint and sick, she flew to her stepfather's room.

Herr Paul was standing in a corner with the utterly disturbed appearance of an easy-going man, visited by the unexpected. His fine shirt-front was crumpled as if his breast had heaved too suddenly under strong emotion; his smoked eyeglasses dangled down his back; his fingers were embedded in his beard. He was fixing his eye on a spot in the floor as though he expected it to explode and blow them to fragments. In another corner Mrs. Decie, with half-closed eyes, was running her finger-tips across her brow.

"What have you said to him?" cried Christian.

Herr Paul regarded her with glassy eyes.

"Mein Gott!" he said. "Your aunt and I!"

"What have you said to him?" repeated Christian.

"The impudence! An anarchist! A beggar!"

"Paul!" murmured Mrs. Decie.

"The outlaw! The fellow!" Herr Paul began to stride about the room.

Quivering from head to foot, Christian cried: "How dared you?" and ran from the room, pushing aside Miss Naylor and Greta, who stood blanched and frightened in the doorway.

Herr Paul stopped in his tramp, and, still with his eyes fixed on the floor, growled:

"A fine thing-hein? What's coming? Will you please tell me? An anarchist—a beggar!"

"Paul!" murmured Mrs. Decie.

"Paul! Paul! And you!" he pointed to Miss Naylor—"Two women with eyes!—hein!"

"There is nothing to be gained by violence," Mrs. Decie murmured, passing her handkerchief across her lips. Miss Naylor, whose thin brown cheeks had flushed, advanced towards him.

"I hope you do not—" she said; "I am sure there was nothing that I could have prevented—I should be glad if that were understood." And, turning with some dignity, the little lady went away, closing the door behind her.

"You hear!" Herr Paul said, violently sarcastic: "nothing she could have prevented! Enfin! Will you please tell me what I am to do?"

"Men of the world"—whose philosophy is a creature of circumstance and accepted things—find any deviation from the path of their convictions dangerous, shocking, and an intolerable bore. Herr Paul had spent his life laughing at convictions; the matter had but to touch him personally, and the tap of laughter was turned off. That any one to whom he was the lawful guardian should marry other than a well-groomed man, properly endowed with goods, properly selected, was beyond expression horrid. From his point of view he had great excuse for horror; and he was naturally unable to judge whether he had excuse for horror from other points of view. His amazement had in it a spice of the pathetic; he was like a child in the presence of a thing that he absolutely could not understand. The interview had left him with a sense of insecurity which he felt to be particularly unfair.

The door was again opened, and Greta flew in, her cheeks flushed, her hair floating behind her, and tears streaming down her cheeks.

"Papa!" she cried, "you have been cruel to Chris. The door is locked; I can hear her crying—why have you been cruel?" Without waiting to be answered, she flew out again.

Herr Paul seized his hair with both his hands: "Good! Very good! My own child, please! What next then?"

Mrs. Decie rose from her chair languidly. "My head is very bad," she said, shading her eyes and speaking in low tones: "It is no use making a fuss—nothing can come of this—he has not a penny. Christian will have nothing till you die, which will not be for a long time yet, if you can but avoid an apoplectic fit!"

At these last words Herr Paul gave a start of real disgust. "Hum!" he muttered; it was as if the world were bent on being brutal to him. Mrs. Decie continued:

"If I know anything of this young man, he will not come here again, after the words you have spoken. As for Christian—you had better talk to Nicholas. I am going to lie down."

Herr Paul nervously fingered the shirt-collar round his stout, short neck.

"Nicholas! Certainly—a good idea. Quelle diable d'afaire!"

'French!' thought Mrs. Decie; 'we shall soon have peace. Poor Christian! I'm sorry! After all, these things are a matter of time and opportunity.' This consoled her a good deal.

But for Christian the hours were a long nightmare of grief and shame, fear and anger. Would he forgive? Would he be true to her? Or would he go away without a word? Since yesterday it was as if she had stepped into another world, and lost it again. In place of that new feeling, intoxicating as wine, what was coming? What bitter; dreadful ending?

A rude entrance this into the life of facts, and primitive emotions!

She let Greta into her room after a time, for the child had begun sobbing; but she would not talk, and sat hour after hour at the window with the air fanning her face, and the pain in her eyes turned to the sky and trees. After one or two attempts at consolation, Greta sank on the floor, and remained there, humbly gazing at her sister in a silence only broken when Christian cleared her throat of tears, and by the song of birds in the garden. In the afternoon she slipped away and did not come back again.

After his interview with Mr. Treffry, Herr Paul took a bath, perfumed himself with precision, and caused it to be clearly understood that, under circumstances such as these, a man's house was not suited for a pig to live in. He shortly afterwards went out to the Kurbaus, and had not returned by dinner-time.

Christian came down for dinner. There were crimson spots in her cheeks, dark circles round her eyes; she behaved, however, as though nothing had happened. Miss Naylor, affected by the kindness of her heart and the shock her system had sustained, rolled a number of bread pills, looking at each as it came, with an air of surprise, and concealing it with difficulty. Mr. Treffry was coughing, and when he talked his voice seemed to rumble even more than usual. Greta was dumb, trying to catch Christian's eye; Mrs. Decie alone seemed at ease. After dinner Mr. Treffry went off to his room, leaning heavily on Christian's shoulder. As he sank into his chair, he said to her:

"Pull yourself together, my dear!" Christian did not answer him.

Outside his room Greta caught her by the sleeve.

"Look!" she whispered, thrusting a piece of paper into Christian's hand. "It is to me from Dr. Edmund, but you must read it."

Christian opened the note, which ran as follows:

"MY PHILOSOPHER AND FRIEND, I received your note, and went to our friend's studio; he was not in, but half an hour ago I stumbled on him in the Platz. He is not quite himself; has had a touch of the sun—nothing serious: I took him to my hotel, where he is in bed. If he will stay there he will be all right in a day or two. In any case he shall not elude my clutches for the present.

"My warm respects to Mistress Christian. Yours in friendship and philosophy,

"EDMUND DAWNEY."

Christian read and re-read this note, then turned to Greta.

"What did you say to Dr. Dawney?"

Greta took back the piece of paper, and replied: "I said:

"'DEAR DR. EDMUND, We are anxious about Herr Harz. We think he is perhaps not very well to-day. We (I and Christian) should like to know. You can tell us. Please shall you? GRETA.'

"That is what I said."

Christian dropped her eyes. "What made you write?"

Greta gazed at her mournfully: "I thought—O Chris! come into the garden. I am so hot, and it is so dull without you!"

Christian bent her head forward and rubbed her cheek against Greta's, then without another word ran upstairs and locked herself into her room. The child stood listening; hearing the key turn in the lock, she sank down on the bottom step and took Scruff in her arms.

Half an hour later Miss Naylor, carrying a candle, found her there fast asleep, with her head resting on the terrier's back, and tear stains on her cheeks....

Mrs. Decie presently came out, also carrying a candle, and went to her brother's room. She stood before his chair, with folded hands.

"Nicholas, what is to be done?"

Mr. Treffry was pouring whisky into a glass.

"Damn it, Con!" he answered; "how should I know?"

"There's something in Christian that makes interference dangerous. I know very well that I've no influence with her at all."

"You're right there, Con," Mr. Treffry replied.

Mrs. Decie's pale eyes, fastened on his face, forced him to look up.

"I wish you would leave off drinking whisky and attend to me. Paul is an element—"

"Paul," Mr. Treffry growled, "is an ass!"

"Paul," pursued Mrs. Decie, "is an element of danger in the situation; any ill-timed opposition of his might drive her to I don't know what. Christian is gentle, she is 'sympathetic' as they say; but thwart her, and she is as obstinate as...."

"You or I! Leave her alone!"

"I understand her character, but I confess that I am at a loss what to do."

"Do nothing!" He drank again.

Mrs. Decie took up the candle.

"Men!" she said with a mysterious intonation; shrugging her shoulders, she walked out.

Mr. Treffry put down his glass.

'Understand?' he thought; 'no, you don't, and I don't. Who understands a young girl? Vapourings, dreams, moonshine I.... What does she see in this painter fellow? I wonder!' He breathed heavily. 'By heavens! I wouldn't have had this happen for a hundred thousand pounds!'

XIII

For many hours after Dawney had taken him to his hotel, Harz was prostrate with stunning pains in the head and neck. He had been all day without food, exposed to burning sun, suffering violent emotion. Movement of any sort caused him such agony that he could only lie in stupor, counting the spots dancing before, his eyes. Dawney did everything for him, and Harz resented in a listless way the intent scrutiny of the doctor's calm, black eyes.

Towards the end of the second day he was able to get up; Dawney found him sitting on the bed in shirt and trousers.

"My son," he said, "you had better tell me what the trouble is—it will do your stubborn carcase good."

"I must go back to work," said Harz.

"Work!" said Dawney deliberately: "you couldn't, if you tried."

"I must."

"My dear fellow, you couldn't tell one colour from another."

"I must be doing something; I can't sit here and think."

Dawney hooked his thumbs into his waistcoat: "You won't see the sun for three days yet, if I can help it."

Harz got up.

"I'm going to my studio to-morrow," he said. "I promise not to go out. I must be where I can see my work. If I can't paint, I can draw; I can feel my brushes, move my things about. I shall go mad if I do nothing."

Dawney took his arm, and walked him up and down.

"I'll let you go," he said, "but give me a chance! It's as much to me to put you straight as it is to you to paint a decent picture. Now go to bed; I'll have a carriage for you to-morrow morning."

Harz sat down on the bed again, and for a long time stayed without moving, his eyes fixed on the floor. The sight of him, so desperate and miserable, hurt the young doctor.

"Can you get to bed by yourself?" he asked at last.

Harz nodded.

"Then, good-night, old chap!" and Dawney left the room.

He took his hat and turned towards the Villa. Between the poplars he stopped to think. The farther trees were fret-worked black against the lingering gold of the sunset; a huge moth, attracted by the tip of his cigar, came fluttering in his face. The music of a concertina rose and fell, like the sighing of some disillusioned spirit. Dawney stood for several minutes staring at the house.

He was shown to Mrs. Decie's room. She was holding a magazine before her eyes, and received him with as much relief as philosophy permitted.

"You are the very person I wanted to see," she said.

He noticed that the magazine she held was uncut.

"You are a young man," pursued Mrs. Decie, "but as my doctor I have a right to your discretion."

Dawney smiled; the features of his broad, clean-shaven face looked ridiculously small on such occasions, but his eyes retained their air of calculation.

"That is so," he answered.

"It is about this unfortunate affair. I understand that Mr. Harz is with you. I want you to use your influence to dissuade him from attempting to see my niece."

"Influence!" said Dawney; "you know Harz!"

Mrs. Decie's voice hardened.

"Everybody," she said, "has his weak points. This young man is open to approach from at least two quarters—his pride is one, his work an other. I am seldom wrong in gauging character; these are his vital spots, and they are of the essence of this matter. I'm sorry for him, of course—but at his age, and living a man's life, these things—" Her smile was extra pale. "I wish you could give me something for my head. It's foolish to worry. Nerves of course! But I can't help it! You know my opinion, Dr. Dawney. That young man will go far if he remains unfettered; he will make a name. You will be doing him a great service if you could show him the affair as it really is—a drag on him, and quite unworthy of his pride! Do help me! You are just the man to do it!"

Dawney threw up his head as if to shake off this impeachment; the curve of his chin thus displayed was imposing in its fulness; altogether he was imposing, having an air of capability.

She struck him, indeed, as really scared; it was as if her mask of smile had become awry, and failed to cover her emotion; and he was puzzled, thinking, 'I wouldn't have believed she had it in her....' "It's not an easy business," he said; "I'll think it over."

"Thank you!" murmured Mrs. Decie. "You are most kind."

Passing the schoolroom, he looked in through the open door. Christian was sitting there. The sight of her face shocked him, it was so white, so resolutely dumb. A book lay on her knees; she was not reading, but staring before her. He thought suddenly: 'Poor thing! If I don't say something to her, I shall be a brute!'

"Miss Devorell," he said: "You can reckon on him."

Christian tried to speak, but her lips trembled so that nothing came forth.

"Good-night," said Dawney, and walked out....

Three days later Harz was sitting in the window of his studio. It was the first day he had found it possible to work, and now, tired out, he stared through the dusk at the slowly lengthening shadows of the rafters. A solitary mosquito hummed, and two house sparrows, who had built beneath the roof, chirruped sleepily. Swallows darted by the window, dipping their blue wings towards the quiet water; a hush had stolen over everything. He fell asleep.

He woke, with a dim impression of some near presence. In the pale glimmer from innumerable stars, the room was full of shadowy shapes. He lit his lantern. The flame darted forth, bickered, then slowly lit up the great room.

"Who's there?"

A rustling seemed to answer. He peered about, went to the doorway, and drew the curtain. A woman's cloaked figure shrank against the wall. Her face was buried in her hands; her arms, from which the cloak fell back, were alone visible.

"Christian?"

She ran past him, and when he had put the lantern down, was standing at the window. She turned quickly to him. "Take me away from here! Let me come with you!"

"Do you mean it?"

"You said you wouldn't give me up!"

"You know what you are doing?"

She made a motion of assent.

"But you don't grasp what this means. Things to bear that you know nothing of—hunger perhaps! Think, even hunger! And your people won't forgive—you'll lose everything."

She shook her head.

"I must choose—it's one thing or the other. I can't give you up! I should be afraid!"

"But, dear; how can you come with me? We can't be married here."

"I am giving my life to you."

"You are too good for me," said Harz. "The life you're going into—may be dark, like that!" he pointed to the window.

A sound of footsteps broke the hush. They could see a figure on the path below. It stopped, seemed to consider, vanished. They heard the sounds of groping hands, of a creaking door, of uncertain feet on the stairs.

Harz seized her hand.

"Quick!" he whispered; "behind this canvas!"

Christian was trembling violently. She drew her hood across her face. The heavy breathing and ejaculations of the visitor were now plainly audible.

"He's there! Quick! Hide!"

She shook her head.

With a thrill at his heart, Harz kissed her, then walked towards the entrance. The curtain was pulled aside.

XIV

It was Herr Paul, holding a cigar in one hand, his hat in the other, and breathing hard.

"Pardon!" he said huskily, "your stairs are steep, and dark! mais en, fin! nous voila! I have ventured to come for a talk." His glance fell on the cloaked figure in the shadow.

"Pardon! A thousand pardons! I had no idea! I beg you to forgive this indiscretion! I may take it you resign pretensions then? You have a lady here—I have nothing more to say; I only beg a million pardons for intruding. A thousand times forgive me! Good-night!"

He bowed and turned to go. Christian stepped forward, and let the hood fall from her head.

"It's I!"

Herr Paul pirouetted.

"Good God!" he stammered, dropping cigar and hat. "Good God!"

The lantern flared suddenly, revealing his crimson, shaking cheeks.

"You came here, at night! You, the daughter of my wife!" His eyes wandered with a dull glare round the room.

"Take care!" cried Harz: "If you say a word against her—"

The two men stared at each other's eyes. And without warning, the lantern flickered and went out. Christian drew the cloak round her again. Herr Paul's voice broke the silence; he had recovered his self-possession.

"Ah! ah!" he said: "Darkness! Tant mieux! The right thing for what we have to say. Since we do not esteem each other, it is well not to see too much."

"Just so," said Harz.

Christian had come close to them. Her pale face and great shining eyes could just be seen through the gloom.

Herr Paul waved his arm; the gesture was impressive, annihilating.

"This is a matter, I believe, between two men," he said, addressing Harz. "Let us come to the point. I will do you the credit to suppose that you have a marriage in view. You know, perhaps, that Miss Devorell has no money till I die?"

"Yes."

"And I am passably young! You have money, then?"

"No."

"In that case, you would propose to live on air?"

"No, to work; it has been done before."

"It is calculated to increase hunger! You are prepared to take Miss Devorell, a young lady accustomed to luxury, into places like—this!" he peered about him, "into places that smell of paint, into the milieu of 'the people,' into the society of Bohemians—who knows? of anarchists, perhaps?"

Harz clenched his hands: "I will answer no more questions."

"In that event, we reach the ultimatum," said Herr Paul. "Listen, Herr Outlaw! If you have not left the country by noon to-morrow, you shall be introduced to the police!"

Christian uttered a cry. For a minute in the gloom the only sound heard was the short, hard breathing of the two men.

Suddenly Harz cried: "You coward, I defy you!"

"Coward!" Herr Paul repeated. "That is indeed the last word. Look to yourself, my friend!"

Stooping and fumbling on the floor, he picked up his hat. Christian had already vanished; the sound of her hurrying footsteps was distinctly audible at the top of the dark stairs. Herr Paul stood still a minute.

"Look to yourself, my dear friend!" he said in a thick voice, groping for the wall. Planting his hat askew on his head, he began slowly to descend the stairs.

XV

Nicholas Treffry sat reading the paper in his room by the light of a lamp with a green shade; on his sound foot the terrier Scruff was asleep and snoring lightly—the dog habitually came down when Greta was in bed, and remained till Mr. Treffry, always the latest member of the household, retired to rest.

Through the long window a little river of light shone out on the veranda tiles, and, flowing past, cut the garden in two.

There was the sound of hurried footsteps, a rustling of draperies; Christian, running through the window, stood before him.

Mr. Treffry dropped his paper, such a fury of passion and alarm shone in the girl's eyes.

"Chris! What is it?"

"Hateful!"

"Chris!"

"Oh! Uncle! He's insulted, threatened! And I love his little finger more than all the world!"

Her passionate voice trembled, her eyes were shining.

Mr. Treffry's profound discomfort found vent in the gruff words: "Sit down!"

"I'll never speak to Father again! Oh! Uncle! I love him!"

Quiet in the extremity of his disturbance, Mr. Treffry leaned forward in his chair, rested his big hands on its arms, and stared at her.

Chris! Here was a woman he did not know! His lips moved under the heavy droop of his moustache. The girl's face had suddenly grown white. She sank down on her knees, and laid her cheek against his hand. He felt it wet; and a lump rose in his throat. Drawing his hand away, he stared at it, and wiped it with his sleeve.

"Don't cry!" he said.

She seized it again and clung to it; that clutch seemed to fill him with sudden rage.

"What's the matter? How the devil can I do anything if you don't tell me?"

She looked up at him. The distress of the last days, the passion and fear of the last hour, the tide of that new life of the spirit and the flesh, stirring within her, flowed out in a stream of words.

When she had finished, there was so dead a silence that the fluttering of a moth round the lamp could be heard plainly.

Mr. Treffry raised himself, crossed the room, and touched the bell. "Tell the groom," he said to Dominique, "to put the horses to, and have 'em round at once; bring my old boots; we drive all night...."

His bent figure looked huge, body and legs outlined by light, head and shoulders towering into shadow. "He shall have a run for his money!" he said. His eyes stared down sombrely at his niece. "It's more than he deserves!—it's more than you deserve, Chris. Sit down there and write to him; tell him to put himself entirely in my hands." He turned his back on her, and went into his bedroom.

Christian rose, and sat down at the writing-table. A whisper startled her. It came from Dominique, who was holding out a pair of boots.

"M'mselle Chris, what is this?—to run about all night?" But Christian did not answer.

"M'mselle Chris, are you ill?" Then seeing her face, he slipped away again.

She finished her letter and went out to the carriage. Mr. Treffry was seated under the hood.

"Shan't want you," he called out to the groom, "Get up, Dominique."

Christian thrust her letter into his hand. "Give him that," she said, clinging to his arm with sudden terror. "Oh! Uncle! do take care!"

"Chris, if I do this for you—" They looked wistfully at one another. Then, shaking his head, Mr. Treffry gathered up the reins.

"Don't fret, my dear, don't fret! Whoa, mare!"

The carriage with a jerk plunged forward into darkness, curved with a crunch of wheels, and vanished, swinging between the black tree-pillars at the entrance....

Christian stood, straining to catch the failing sound of the hoofs.

Down the passage came a flutter of white garments; soft limbs were twined about her, some ends of hair fell on her face.

"What is it, Chris? Where have you been? Where is Uncle Nic going? Tell me!"

Christian tore herself away. "I don't know," she cried, "I know nothing!"

Greta stroked her face. "Poor Chris!" she murmured. Her bare feet gleamed, her hair shone gold against her nightdress. "Come to bed, poor Chris!"

Christian laughed. "You little white moth! Feel how hot I am! You'll burn your wings!"

XVI

Harz had lain down, fully dressed. He was no longer angry, but felt that he would rather die than yield. Presently he heard footsteps coming up the stairs.

"M'sieu!"

It was the voice of Dominique, whose face, illumined by a match, wore an expression of ironical disgust.

"My master," he said, "makes you his compliments; he says there is no time to waste. You are to please come and drive with him!"

"Your master is very kind. Tell him I'm in bed."

"Ah, M'sieu," said Dominique, grimacing, "I must not go back with such an answer. If you would not come, I was to give you this."

Harz broke the seal and read Christian's letter.

"I will come," he said.

A clock was striking as they went out through the gate. From within the dark cave of the phaeton hood Mr. Treffry said gruffly: "Come along, sir!"

Harz flung his knapsack in, and followed.

His companion's figure swayed, the whiplash slid softly along the flank of the off horse, and, as the carriage rattled forward, Mr. Treffry called out, as if by afterthought: "Hallo, Dominique!" Dominque's voice, shaken and ironical, answered from behind: "M'v'la, M'sieu!"

In the long street of silent houses, men sitting in the lighted cafes turned with glasses at their lips to stare after the carriage. The narrow river of the sky spread suddenly to a vast, limpid ocean tremulous with stars. They had turned into the road for Italy.

Mr. Treffry took a pull at his horses. "Whoa, mare! Dogged does it!" and the near horse, throwing up her head, whinnied; a fleck of foam drifted into Harz's face.

The painter had come on impulse; because Christian had told him to, not of his own free will. He was angry with himself, wounded in self-esteem, for having allowed any one to render him this service. The smooth swift movement through velvet blackness splashed on either hand with the flying lamp-light; the strong sweet air blowing in his face-air that had kissed the tops of mountains and stolen their spirit; the snort and snuffle of the horses, and crisp rattling of their hoofs—all this soon roused in him another feeling. He looked at Mr. Treffry's profile, with its tufted chin; at the grey road adventuring in darkness; at the purple mass of mountains piled above it. All seemed utterly unreal.

As if suddenly aware that he had a neighbour, Mr. Treffry turned his head. "We shall do better than this presently," he said, "bit of a slope coming. Haven't had 'em out for three days. Whoa-mare! Steady!"

"Why are you taking this trouble for me?" asked Harz.

"I'm an old chap, Mr. Harz, and an old chap may do a stupid thing once in a while!"

"You are very good," said Harz, "but I want no favours."

Mr. Treffry stared at him.

"Just so," he said drily, "but you see there's my niece to be thought of. Look here! We're not at the frontier yet, Mr. Harz, by forty miles; it's long odds we don't get there—so, don't spoil sport!" He pointed to the left.

Harz caught the glint of steel. They were already crossing the railway. The sigh of the telegraph wires fluttered above them.

"Hear 'em," said Mr. Treffry, "but if we get away up the mountains, we'll do yet!" They had begun to rise, the speed slackened. Mr. Treffry rummaged out a flask.

"Not bad stuff, Mr. Harz—try it. You won't? Mother's milk! Fine night, eh?" Below them the valley was lit by webs of milky mist like the glimmer of dew on grass.

These two men sitting side by side—unlike in face, age, stature, thought, and life—began to feel drawn towards each other, as if, in the rolling of the wheels, the snorting of the horses, the huge dark space, the huge uncertainty, they had found something they could enjoy in common. The steam from the horses' flanks and nostrils enveloped them with an odour as of glue.

"You smoke, Mr. Harz?"

Harz took the proffered weed, and lighted it from the glowing tip of Mr. Treffry's cigar, by light of which his head and hat looked like some giant mushroom. Suddenly the wheels jolted on a rubble of loose stones; the carriage was swung sideways. The scared horses, straining asunder, leaped forward, and sped downwards, in the darkness.

Past rocks, trees, dwellings, past a lighted house that gleamed and vanished. With a clink and clatter, a flirt of dust and pebbles, and the side lamps throwing out a frisky orange blink, the carriage dashed down, sinking and rising like a boat crossing billows. The world seemed to rock and sway; to dance up, and be flung flat again. Only the stars stood still.

Mr. Treffry, putting on the brake, muttered apologetically: "A little out o'hand!"

Suddenly with a headlong dive, the carriage swayed as if it would fly in pieces, slithered along, and with a jerk steadied itself. Harz lifted his voice in a shout of pure excitement. Mr. Treffry let out a short shaky howl, and from behind there rose a wail. But the hill was over and the startled horses were cantering with a free, smooth motion. Mr. Treffry and Harz looked at each other.

XVII

Mr. Treffry said with a sort of laugh: "Near go, eh? You drive? No? That's a pity! Broken most of my bones at the game—nothing like it!" Each felt a kind of admiration for the other that he had not felt before. Presently Mr. Treffry began: "Look here, Mr. Harz, my niece is a slip of a thing, with all a young girl's notions! What have you got to give her, eh? Yourself? That's surely not enough; mind this—six months after marriage we all turn out much the same—a selfish lot! Not to mention this anarchist affair!

"You're not of her blood, nor of her way of life, nor anything—it's taking chances—and—" his hand came down on the young man's knee, "I'm fond of her, you see."

"If you were in my place," said Harz, "would you give her up?"

Mr. Treffry groaned. "Lord knows!"

"Men have made themselves before now. For those who don't believe in failure, there's no such thing. Suppose she does suffer a little? Will it do her any harm? Fair weather love is no good."

Mr. Treffry sighed.

"Brave words, sir! You'll pardon me if I'm too old to understand 'em when they're used about my niece."

He pulled the horses up, and peered into the darkness. "We're going through this bit quietly; if they lose track of us here so much the better. Dominique! put out the lamps. Soho, my beauties!" The horses paced forward at a walk the muffled beat of their hoofs in the dust hardly broke the hush. Mr. Treffry pointed to the left: "It'll be another thirty-five miles to the frontier."

They passed the whitewashed houses, and village church with its sentinel cypress-trees. A frog was croaking in a runlet; there was a faint spicy scent of lemons. But nothing stirred.

It was wood now on either side, the high pines, breathing their fragrance out into the darkness, and, like ghosts amongst them, the silver stems of birch-trees.

Mr. Treffry said gruffly: "You won't give her up? Her happiness means a lot to me."

"To you!" said Harz: "to him! And I am nothing! Do you think I don't care for her happiness? Is it a crime for me to love her?"

"Almost, Mr. Harz—considering...."

"Considering that I've no money! Always money!"

To this sneer Mr. Treffry made no answer, clucking to his horses.

"My niece was born and bred a lady," he said at last. "I ask you plainly What position have you got to give her?"

"If she marries me," said Harz, "she comes into my world. You think that I'm a common...."

Mr. Treffry shook his head: "Answer my question, young man."

But the painter did not answer it, and silence fell.

A light breeze had sprung up; the whispering in the trees, the rolling of the wheels in this night progress, the pine-drugged air, sent Harz to sleep. When he woke it was to the same tune, varied by Mr. Treffry's uneasy snoring; the reins were hanging loose, and, peering out, he saw Dominique shuffling along at the horses' heads. He joined him, and, one on each side, they plodded up and up. A haze had begun to bathe the trees, the stars burnt dim, the air was colder. Mr. Treffry woke coughing. It was like some long nightmare, this interminable experience of muffled sounds and shapes, of perpetual motion, conceived, and carried out in darkness. But suddenly the day broke. Heralded by the snuffle of the horses, light began glimmering over a chaos of lines and shadows, pale as mother-o'-pearl. The stars faded, and in a smouldering zigzag the dawn fled along the mountain tops, flinging out little isles of cloud. From a lake, curled in a hollow like a patch of smoke, came the cry of a water-bird. A cuckoo started a soft mocking; and close to the carriage a lark flew up. Beasts and men alike stood still, drinking in the air-sweet with snows and dew, and vibrating faintly with the running of the water and the rustling of the leaves.

The night had played sad tricks with Mr. Nicholas Treffry; his hat was grey with dust; his cheeks brownish-purple, there were heavy pouches beneath his eyes, which stared painfully.

"We'll call a halt," he said, "and give the gees their grub, poor things. Can you find some water, Mr. Harz? There's a rubber bucket in behind.

"Can't get about myself this morning; make that lazy fellow of mine stir his stumps."

Harz saw that he had drawn off one of his boots, and stretched the foot out on a cushion.

"You're not fit to go farther," he said; "you're ill."

"Ill!" replied Mr. Treffry; "not a bit of it!"

Harz looked at him, then catching up the bucket, made off in search of water. When he came back the horses were feeding from an india-rubber trough slung to the pole; they stretched their heads towards the bucket, pushing aside each other's noses.

The flame in the east had died, but the tops of the larches were bathed in a gentle radiance; and the peaks ahead were like amber. Everywhere were threads of water, threads of snow, and little threads of dewy green, glistening like gossamer.

Mr. Treffry called out: "Give me your arm, Mr. Harz; I'd like to shake the reefs out of me. When one comes to stand over at the knees, it's no such easy matter, eh?" He groaned as he put his foot down, and gripped the young man's shoulder as in a vise. Presently he lowered himself on to a stone.

"'All over now!' as Chris would say when she was little; nasty temper she had too—kick and scream on the floor! Never lasted long though.... 'Kiss her! take her up! show her the pictures!' Amazing fond of pictures Chris was!" He looked dubiously at Harz; then took a long pull at his flask. "What would the doctor say? Whisky at four in the morning! Well! Thank the Lord Doctors aren't always with us." Sitting on the stone, with one hand pressed against his side, and the other tilting up the flask, he was grey from head to foot.

Harz had dropped on to another stone. He, too, was worn out by the excitement and fatigue, coming so soon after his illness. His head was whirling, and the next thing he remembered was a tree walking at him, turning round, yellow from the roots up; everything seemed yellow, even his own feet. Somebody opposite to him was jumping up and down, a grey bear—with a hat—Mr. Treffry! He cried: "Ha-alloo!" And the figure seemed to fall and disappear....

When Harz came to himself a hand was pouring liquor into his mouth, and a wet cloth was muffled round his brows; a noise of humming and hoofs seemed familiar. Mr. Treffry loomed up alongside, smoking a cigar; he was muttering: "A low trick, Paul—bit of my mind!" Then, as if a curtain had been snatched aside, the vision before Harz cleared again. The carriage was winding between uneven, black-eaved houses, past doorways from which goats and cows were coming out, with bells on their necks. Black-eyed boys, and here and there a drowsy man with a long, cherry-stemmed pipe between his teeth, stood aside to stare.

Mr. Treffry seemed to have taken a new lease of strength; like an angry old dog, he stared from side to side. "My bone!" he seemed to say: "let's see who's going to touch it!"

The last house vanished, glowing in the early sunshine, and the carriage with its trail of dust became entombed once more in the gloom of tall trees, along a road that cleft a wilderness of mossgrown rocks, and dewy stems, through which the sun had not yet driven paths.

Dominique came round to them, bearing appearance of one who has seen better days, and a pot of coffee brewed on a spirit lamp. Breakfast—he said—was served!

The ears of the horses were twitching with fatigue. Mr. Treffry said sadly: "If I can see this through, you can. Get on, my beauties!"

As soon as the sun struck through the trees, Mr. Treffry's strength ebbed again. He seemed to suffer greatly; but did not complain. They had reached the pass at last, and the unchecked sunlight was streaming down with a blinding glare.

"Jump up!" Mr. Treffry cried out. "We'll make a finish of it!" and he gave the reins a jerk. The horses flung up their heads, and the bleak pass with its circling crown of jagged peaks soon slipped away.

Between the houses on the very top, they passed at a slow trot; and soon began slanting down the other side. Mr. Treffry brought them to a halt where a mule track joined the road.

"That's all I can do for you; you'd better leave me here," he said. "Keep this track down to the river— go south—you'll be in Italy in a couple of hours. Get rail at Feltre. Money? Yes? Well!" He held out his hand; Harz gripped it.

"Give her up, eh?"

Harz shook his head.

"No? Then it's 'pull devil, pull baker,' between us. Good-bye, and good luck to you!" And mustering his strength for a last attempt at dignity, Mr. Treffry gathered up the reins.

Harz watched his figure huddled again beneath the hood. The carriage moved slowly away.

XVIII

At Villa Rubein people went about, avoiding each other as if detected in conspiracy. Miss Naylor, who for an inscrutable reason had put on her best frock, a purple, relieved at the chest with bird's-eye blue, conveyed an impression of trying to count a chicken which ran about too fast. When Greta asked what she had lost she was heard to mutter: "Mr.—Needlecase."

Christian, with big circles round her eyes, sat silent at her little table. She had had no sleep. Herr Paul coming into the room about noon gave her a furtive look and went out again; after this he went to his bedroom, took off all his clothes, flung them passionately one by one into a footbath, and got into bed.

"I might be a criminal!" he muttered to himself, while the buttons of his garments rattled on the bath.

"Am I her father? Have I authority? Do I know the world? Bsssss! I might be a frog!"

Mrs. Decie, having caused herself to be announced, found him smoking a cigar, and counting the flies on the ceiling.

"If you have really done this, Paul," she said in a restrained voice, "you have done a very unkind thing, and what is worse, you have made us all ridiculous. But perhaps you have not done it?"

"I have done it," cried Herr Paul, staring dreadfully: "I have done it, I tell you, I have done it—"

"Very well, you have done it—and why, pray? What conceivable good was there in it? I suppose you know that Nicholas has driven him to the frontier? Nicholas is probably more dead than alive by this time; you know his state of health."

Herr Paul's fingers ploughed up his beard.

"Nicholas is mad—and the girl is mad! Leave me alone! I will not be made angry; do you understand? I will not be worried—I am not fit for it." His prominent brown eyes stared round the room, as if looking for a way of escape.

"If I may prophesy, you will be worried a good deal," said Mrs. Decie coldly, "before you have finished with this affair."

The anxious, uncertain glance which Herr Paul gave her at these words roused an unwilling feeling of compunction in her.

"You are not made for the outraged father of the family," she said. "You had better give up the attitude, Paul; it does not suit you."

Herr Paul groaned.

"I suppose it is not your fault," she added.

Just then the door was opened, and Fritz, with an air of saying the right thing, announced:

"A gentleman of the police to see you, sir."

Herr Paul bounded.

"Keep him out!" he cried.

Mrs. Decie, covering her lips, disappeared with a rustling of silk; in her place stood a stiff man in blue....

Thus the morning dragged itself away without any one being able to settle to anything, except Herr Paul, who was settled in bed. As was fitting in a house that had lost its soul, meals were neglected, even by the dog.

About three o'clock a telegram came for Christian, containing these words: "All right; self returns to-morrow. Treffry." After reading it she put on her hat and went out, followed closely by Greta, who, when she thought that she would not be sent away, ran up from behind and pulled her by the sleeve.

"Let me come, Chris—I shall not talk."

The two girls walked on together. When they had gone some distance Christian said:

"I'm going to get his pictures, and take charge of them!"

"Oh!" said Greta timidly.

"If you are afraid," said Christian, "you had better go back home."

"I am not afraid, Chris," said Greta meekly.

Neither girl spoke again till they had taken the path along the wall. Over the tops of the vines the heat was dancing.

"The sun-fairies are on the vines!" murmured Greta to herself.

At the old house they stopped, and Christian, breathing quickly, pushed the door; it was immovable.

"Look!" said Greta, "they have screwed it!" She pointed out three screws with a rosy-tipped forefinger.

Christian stamped her foot.

"We mustn't stand here," she said; "let's sit on that bench and think."

"Yes," murmured Greta, "let us think." Dangling an end of hair, she regarded Christian with her wide blue eyes.

"I can't make any plan," Christian cried at last, "while you stare at me like that."

"I was thinking," said Greta humbly, "if they have screwed it up, perhaps we shall screw it down again; there is the big screw-driver of Fritz."

"It would take a long time; people are always passing."

"People do not pass in the evening," murmured Greta, "because the gate at our end is always shut."

Christian rose.

"We will come this evening, just before the gate is shut."

"But, Chris, how shall we get back again?"

"I don't know; I mean to have the pictures."

"It is not a high gate," murmured Greta.

After dinner the girls went to their room, Greta bearing with her the big screw-driver of Fritz. At dusk they slipped downstairs and out.

They arrived at the old house, and stood, listening, in the shadow of the doorway. The only sounds were those of distant barking dogs, and of the bugles at the barracks.

"Quick!" whispered Christian; and Greta, with all the strength of her small hands, began to turn the screws. It was some time before they yielded; the third was very obstinate, till Christian took the screw-driver and passionately gave the screw a starting twist.

"It is like a pig—that one," said Greta, rubbing her wrists mournfully.

The opened door revealed the gloom of the dank rooms and twisting staircase, then fell to behind them with a clatter.

Greta gave a little scream, and caught her sister's dress.

"It is dark," she gasped; "O Chris! it is dark!"

Christian groped for the bottom stair, and Greta felt her arm shaking.

"Suppose there is a man to keep guard! O Chris! suppose there are bats!"

"You are a baby!" Christian answered in a trembling voice. "You had better go home!"

Greta choked a little in the dark.

"I am—not—going home, but I'm afraid of bats. O Chris! aren't you afraid?"

"Yes," said Christian, "but I'm going to have the pictures."

Her cheeks were burning; she was trembling all over. Having found the bottom step she began to mount with Greta clinging to her skirts.

The haze above inspired a little courage in the child, who, of all things, hated darkness. The blanket across the doorway of the loft had been taken down, there was nothing to veil the empty room.

"Nobody here, you see," said Christian.

"No-o," whispered Greta, running to the window, and clinging to the wall, like one of the bats she dreaded.

"But they have been here!" cried Christian angrily. "They have broken this." She pointed to the fragments of a plaster cast that had been thrown down.

Out of the corner she began to pull the canvases set in rough, wooden frames, dragging them with all her strength.

"Help me!" she cried; "it will be dark directly."

They collected a heap of sketches and three large pictures, piling them before the window, and peering at them in the failing light.

Greta said ruefully:

"O Chris! they are heavy ones; we shall never carry them, and the gate is shut now!"

Christian took a pointed knife from the table.

"I shall cut them out of the frames," she said. "Listen! What's that?"

It was the sound of whistling, which stopped beneath the window. The girls, clasping each other's hands, dropped on their knees.

"Hallo!" cried a voice.

Greta crept to the window, and, placing her face level with the floor, peered over.

"It is only Dr. Edmund; he doesn't know, then," she whispered; "I shall call him; he is going away!" cried Christian catching her sister's—"Don't!" cried Christian catching her sister's dress.

"He would help us," Greta said reproachfully, "and it would not be so dark if he were here."

Christian's cheeks were burning.

"I don't choose," she said, and began handling the pictures, feeling their edges with her knife.

"Chris! Suppose anybody came?"

"The door is screwed," Christian answered absently.

"O Chris! We screwed it unscrewed; anybody who wishes shall come!"

Christian, leaning her chin in her hands, gazed at her thoughtfully.

"It will take a long time to cut these pictures out carefully; or, perhaps I can get them out without cutting. You must screw me up and go home. In the morning you must come early, when the gate is open, unscrew me again, and help carry the pictures."

Greta did not answer at once. At last she shook her head violently.

"I am afraid," she gasped.

"We can't both stay here all night," said Christian; "if any one comes to our room there will be nobody to answer. We can't lift these pictures over the gate. One of us must go back; you can climb over the gate—there is nothing to be afraid of."

Greta pressed her hands together.

"Do you want the pictures badly, Chris?"

Christian nodded.

"Very badly?"

"Yes—yes—yes!"

Greta remained sitting where she was, shivering violently, as a little animal shivers when it scents danger. At last she rose.

"I am going," she said in a despairing voice. At the doorway she turned.

"If Miss Naylor shall ask me where you are, Chris, I shall be telling her a story."

Christian started.

"I forgot that—O Greta, I am sorry! I will go instead."

Greta took another step—a quick one.

"I shall die if I stay here alone," she said; "I can tell her that you are in bed; you must go to bed here, Chris, so it shall be true after all."

Christian threw her arms about her.

"I am so sorry, darling; I wish I could go instead. But if you have to tell a lie, I would tell a straight one."

"Would you?" said Greta doubtfully.

"Yes."

"I think," said Greta to herself, beginning to descend the stairs, "I think I will tell it in my way." She shuddered and went on groping in the darkness.

Christian listened for the sound of the screws. It came slowly, threatening her with danger and solitude.

Sinking on her knees she began to work at freeing the canvas of a picture. Her heart throbbed distressfully; at the stir of wind-breath or any distant note of clamour she stopped, and held her breathing. No sounds came near. She toiled on, trying only to think that she was at the very spot where last night his arms had been round her. How long ago it seemed! She was full of vague terror, overmastered by the darkness, dreadfully alone. The new glow of resolution seemed suddenly to have died down in her heart, and left her cold.

She would never be fit to be his wife, if at the first test her courage failed! She set her teeth; and suddenly she felt a kind of exultation, as if she too were entering into life, were knowing something within herself that she had never known before. Her fingers hurt, and the pain even gave pleasure; her cheeks were burning; her breath came fast. They could not stop her now! This feverish task in darkness was her baptism into life. She finished; and rolling the pictures very carefully, tied them with cord. She had done something for him! Nobody could take that from her! She had a part of him! This night had made him hers! They might do their worst! She lay down on his mattress and soon fell asleep....

She was awakened by Scruff's tongue against her face. Greta was standing by her side.

"Wake up, Chris! The gate is open!"

In the cold early light the child seemed to glow with warmth and colour; her eyes were dancing.

"I am not afraid now; Scruff and I sat up all night, to catch the morning—I—think it was fun; and O Chris!" she ended with a rueful gleam in her eyes, "I told it."

Christian hugged her.

"Come—quick! There is nobody about. Are those the pictures?"

Each supporting an end, the girls carried the bundle downstairs, and set out with their corpse-like burden along the wall-path between the river and the vines.

XIX

Hidden by the shade of rose-bushes Greta lay stretched at length, cheek on arm, sleeping the sleep of the unrighteous. Through the flowers the sun flicked her parted lips with kisses, and spilled the withered petals on her. In a denser islet of shade, Scruff lay snapping at a fly. His head lolled drowsily in the middle of a snap, and snapped in the middle of a loll.

At three o'clock Miss Naylor too came out, carrying a basket and pair of scissors. Lifting her skirts to avoid the lakes of water left by the garden hose, she stopped in front of a rose-bush, and began to snip off the shrivelled flowers. The little lady's silvered head and thin, brown face sustained the shower of sunlight unprotected, and had a gentle dignity in their freedom.

Presently, as the scissors flittered in and out of the leaves, she, began talking to herself.

"If girls were more like what they used to be, this would not have happened. Perhaps we don't understand; it's very easy to forget." Burying her nose and lips in a rose, she sniffed. "Poor dear girl! It's such a pity his father is—a—"

"A farmer," said a sleepy voice behind the rosebush.

Miss Naylor leaped. "Greta! How you startled me! A farmer—that is—an—an agriculturalist!"

"A farmer with vineyards—he told us, and he is not ashamed. Why is it a pity, Miss Naylor?"

Miss Naylor's lips looked very thin.

"For many reasons, of which you know nothing."

"That is what you always say," pursued the sleepy voice; "and that is why, when I am to be married, there shall also be a pity."

"Greta!" Miss Naylor cried, "it is not proper for a girl of your age to talk like that."

"Why?" said Greta. "Because it is the truth?"

Miss Naylor made no reply to this, but vexedly cut off a sound rose, which she hastily picked up and regarded with contrition. Greta spoke again:

"Chris said: 'I have got the pictures, I shall tell her'; but I shall tell you instead, because it was I that told the story."

Miss Naylor stared, wrinkling her nose, and holding the scissors wide apart....

"Last night," said Greta slowly, "I and Chris went to his studio and took his pictures, and so, because the gate was shut, I came back to tell it; and when you asked me where Chris was, I told it; because she was in the studio all night, and I and Scruff sat up all night, and in the morning we brought the pictures, and hid them under our beds, and that is why—we—are—so—sleepy."

Over the rose-bush Miss Naylor peered down at her; and though she was obliged to stand on tiptoe this did not altogether destroy her dignity.

"I am surprised at you, Greta; I am surprised at Christian, more surprised at Christian. The world seems upside down."

Greta, a sunbeam entangled in her hair, regarded her with inscrutable, innocent eyes.

"When you were a girl, I think you would be sure to be in love," she murmured drowsily.

Miss Naylor, flushing deeply, snipped off a particularly healthy bud.

"And so, because you are not married, I think—"

The scissors hissed.

Greta nestled down again. "I think it is wicked to cut off all the good buds," she said, and shut her eyes.

Miss Naylor continued to peer across the rosebush; but her thin face, close to the glistening leaves, had become oddly soft, pink, and girlish. At a deeper breath from Greta, the little lady put down her basket, and began to pace the lawn, followed dubiously by Scruff. It was thus that Christian came on them.

Miss Naylor slipped her arm into the girl's and though she made no sound, her lips kept opening and shutting, like the beak of a bird contemplating a worm.

Christian spoke first:

"Miss Naylor, I want to tell you please—"

"Oh, my dear! I know; Greta has been in the confessional before you." She gave the girl's arm a squeeze. "Isn't it a lovely day? Did you ever see 'Five Fingers' look so beautiful?" And she pointed to the great peaks of the Funffingerspitze glittering in the sun like giant crystals.

"I like them better with clouds about them."

"Well," agreed Miss Naylor nervously, "they certainly are nicer with clouds about them. They look almost hot and greasy, don't they.... My dear!" she went on, giving Christian's arm a dozen little squeezes, "we all of us—that is, we all of us—"

Christian turned her eyes away.

"My dear," Miss Naylor tried again, "I am far—that is, I mean, to all of us at some time or another—and then you see—well—it is hard!"

Christian kissed the gloved hand resting on her arm. Miss Naylor bobbed her head; a tear trickled off her nose.

"Do let us wind your skein of woof!" she said with resounding gaiety.

Some half-hour later Mrs. Decie called Christian to her room.

"My dear!" she said; "come here a minute; I have a message for you."

Christian went with an odd, set look about her mouth.

Her aunt was sitting, back to the light, tapping a bowl of goldfish with the tip of a polished finger-nail; the room was very cool. She held a letter out. "Your uncle is not coming back tonight."

Christian took the letter. It was curtly worded, in a thin, toppling hand:

"DEAR CON—Can't get back to-night. Sending Dominique for things. Tell Christian to come over with him for night if possible.—Yr. aff. brother, NICLS. TREFFRY."

"Dominique has a carriage here," said Mrs. Decie. "You will have nice time to catch the train. Give my love to your uncle. You must take Barbi with you, I insist on that." She rose from her chair and held Christian's hand: "My dear! You look very tired—very! Almost ill. I don't like to see you look like that. Come!" She thrust her pale lips forward, and kissed the girl's paler cheek.

Then as Christian left the room she sank back in her chair, with creases in her forehead, and began languidly to cut a magazine. 'Poor Christian!' she thought, 'how hardly she does take it! I am sorry for her; but perhaps it's just as well, as things are turning out. Psychologically it is interesting!'

Christian found her things packed, and the two servants waiting. In a few minutes they were driving to the station. She made Dominique take the seat opposite.

"Well?" she asked him.

Dominique's eyebrows twitched, he smiled deprecatingly.

"M'mselle, Mr. Treffry told me to hold my tongue."

"But you can tell me, Dominique; Barbi can't understand."

"To you, then, M'mselle," said Dominique, as one who accepts his fate; "to you, then, who will doubtless forget all that I shall tell you—my master is not well; he has terrible pain here; he has a cough; he is not well at all; not well at all."

A feeling of dismay seized on the girl.

"We were a caravan for all that night," Dominique resumed. "In the morning by noon we ceased to be a caravan; Signor Harz took a mule path; he will be in Italy—certainly in Italy. As for us, we stayed at San Martino, and my master went to bed. It was time; I had much trouble with his clothes, his legs were swollen. In the afternoon came a signor of police, on horseback, red and hot; I persuaded him that we were at Paneveggio, but as we were not, he came back angry—Mon Die! as angry as a cat. It was not good to meet him—when he was with my master I was outside. There was much noise. I do not know what passed, but at last the signor came out through the door, and went away in a hurry." Dominique's features were fixed in a sardonic grin; he rubbed the palm of one hand with the finger of the other. "Mr. Treffry made me give him whisky afterwards, and he had no money to pay the bill—that I know because I paid it. Well, M'mselle, to-day he would be dressed and very slowly we came as far as Auer; there he could do no more, so went to bed. He is not well at all."

Christian was overwhelmed by forebodings; the rest of the journey was made in silence, except when Barbi, a country girl, filled with the delirium of railway travel, sighed: "Ach! gnadige Fraulein!" looking at Christian with pleasant eyes.

At once, on arriving at the little hostel, Christian went to see her uncle. His room was darkened, and smelt of beeswax.

"Ah! Chris," he said, "glad to see you."

In a blue flannel gown, with a rug over his feet, he was lying on a couch lengthened artificially by chairs; the arm he reached out issued many inches from its sleeve, and showed the corded veins of the wrist. Christian, settling his pillows, looked anxiously into his eyes.

"I'm not quite the thing, Chris," said Mr. Treffry. "Somehow, not quite the thing. I'll come back with you to-morrow."

"Let me send for Dr. Dawney, Uncle?"

"No—no! Plenty of him when I get home. Very good young fellow, as doctors go, but I can't stand his puddin's—slops and puddin's, and all that trumpery medicine on the top. Send me Dominique, my dear—I'll put myself to rights a bit!" He fingered his unshaven cheek, and clutched the gown together on his chest. "Got this from the landlord. When you come back we'll have a little talk!"

He was asleep when she came into the room an hour later. Watching his uneasy breathing, she wondered what it was that he was going to say.

He looked ill! And suddenly she realised that her thoughts were not of him.... When she was little he would take her on his back; he had built cocked hats for her and paper boats; had taught her to ride; slid her between his knees; given her things without number; and taken his payment in kisses. And now he was ill, and she was not thinking of him! He had been all that was most dear to her, yet before her eyes would only come the vision of another.

Mr. Treffry woke suddenly. "Not been asleep, have I? The beds here are infernal hard."

"Uncle Nic, won't you give me news of him?"

Mr. Treffry looked at her, and Christian could not bear that look.

"He's safe into Italy; they aren't very keen after him, it's so long ago; I squared 'em pretty easily. Now, look here, Chris!"

Christian came close; he took her hand.

"I'd like to see you pull yourself together. 'Tisn't so much the position; 'tisn't so much the money; because after all there's always mine—" Christian shook her head. "But," he went on with shaky emphasis, "there's the difference of blood, and that's a serious thing; and there's this anarch—this political affair; and there's the sort of life, an' that's a serious thing; but—what I'm coming to is this, Chris—there's the man!"

Christian drew away her hand. Mr. Treffry went on:

"Ah! yes. I'm an old chap and fond of you, but I must speak out what I think. He's got pluck, he's strong, he's in earnest; but he's got a damned hot temper, he's an egotist, and—he's not the man for you. If you marry him, as sure as I lie here, you'll be sorry for it. You're not your father's child for nothing; nice fellow as ever lived, but soft as butter. If you take this chap, it'll be like mixing earth and ironstone, and they don't blend!" He dropped his head back on the pillows, and stretching out his hand, repeated wistfully: "Take my word for it, my dear, he's not the man for you."

Christian, staring at the wall beyond, said quietly: "I can't take any one's word for that."

"Ah!" muttered Mr. Treffry, "you're obstinate enough, but obstinacy isn't strength.

"You'll give up everything to him, you'll lick his shoes; and you'll never play anything but second fiddle in his life. He'll always be first with himself, he and his work, or whatever he calls painting pictures; and some day you'll find that out. You won't like it, and I don't like it for you, Chris, and that's flat."

He wiped his brow where the perspiration stood in beads.

Christian said: "You don't understand; you don't believe in him; you don't see! If I do come after his work—if I do give him everything, and he can't give all back—I don't care! He'll give what he can; I don't want any more. If you're afraid of the life for me, uncle, if you think it'll be too hard—"

Mr. Treffry bowed his head. "I do, Chris."

"Well, then, I hate to be wrapped in cotton wool; I want to breathe. If I come to grief, it's my own affair; nobody need mind."

Mr. Treffry's fingers sought his beard. "Ah! yes. Just so!"

Christian sank on her knees.

"Oh! Uncle! I'm a selfish beast!"

Mr. Treffry laid his hand against her cheek. "I think I could do with a nap," he said.

Swallowing a lump in her throat, she stole out of the room.

XX

By a stroke of Fate Mr. Treffry's return to Villa Rubein befell at the psychological moment when Herr Paul, in a suit of rather too bright blue, was starting for Vienna.

As soon as he saw the carriage appear between the poplars he became as pensive as a boy caught in the act of stealing cherries. Pitching his hatbox to Fritz, he recovered himself, however, in time to whistle while Mr. Treffry was being assisted into the house. Having forgotten his anger, he was only anxious now to smooth out its after effects; in the glances he cast at Christian and his brother-in-law there was a kind of shamed entreaty which seemed to say: "For goodness' sake, don't worry me about that business again! Nothing's come of it, you see!"

He came forward: "Ah! Mon cher! So you return; I put off my departure, then. Vienna must wait for me—that poor Vienna!"

But noticing the extreme feebleness of Mr. Treffry's advance, he exclaimed with genuine concern:

"What is it? You're ill? My God!" After disappearing for five minutes, he came back with a whitish liquid in a glass.

"There!" he said, "good for the gout—for a cough—for everything!"

Mr. Treffry sniffed, drained the glass, and sucked his moustache.

"Ah!" he said. "No doubt! But it's uncommonly like gin, Paul." Then turning to Christian, he said: "Shake hands, you two!"

Christian looked from one to the other, and at last held out her hand to Herr Paul, who brushed it with his moustache, gazing after her as she left the room with a queer expression.

"My dear!" he began, "you support her in this execrable matter? You forget my position, you make me ridiculous. I have been obliged to go to bed in my own house, absolutely to go to bed, because I was in danger of becoming funny."

"Look here, Paul!" Mr. Treffry said gruffly, "if any one's to bully Chris, it's I."

"In that case," returned Herr Paul sarcastically, "I will go to Vienna."

"You may go to the devil!" said Mr. Treffry; "and I'll tell you what—in my opinion it was low to set the police on that young chap; a low, dirty trick."

Herr Paul divided his beard carefully in two, took his seat on the very edge of an arm-chair, and placing his hands on his parted knees, said:

"I have regretted it since—mais, que diable! He called me a coward—it is very hot weather!—there were drinks at the Kurhaus—I am her guardian—the affair is a very beastly one—there were more drinks—I was a little enfin!" He shrugged his shoulders. "Adieu, my dear; I shall be some time in Vienna; I need rest!" He rose and went to the door; then he turned, and waved his cigar. "Adieu! Be good; get well! I will buy you some cigars up there." And going out, he shut the door on any possibility of answer.

Mr. Treffry lay back amongst his cushions. The clock ticked; pigeons cooed on the veranda; a door opened in the distance, and for a moment a treble voice was heard. Mr. Treffry's head drooped forward; across his face, gloomy and rugged, fell a thin line of sunlight.

The clock suddenly stopped ticking, and outside, in mysterious accord, the pigeons rose with a great fluttering of wings, and flew off'. Mr. Treffry made a startled, heavy movement. He tried to get on to his feet and reach the bell, but could not, and sat on the side of the couch with drops of sweat rolling off his forehead, and his hands clawing his chest. There was no sound at all throughout the house. He looked about him, and tried to call, but again could not. He tried once more to reach the bell, and, failing, sat still, with a thought that made him cold.

"I'm done for," he muttered. "By George! I believe I'm done for this time!" A voice behind him said:

"Can we have a look at you, sir?"

"Ah! Doctor, bear a hand, there's a good fellow."

Dawney propped him against the cushions, and loosened his shirt. Receiving no answer to his questions, he stepped alarmed towards the bell. Mr. Treffry stopped him with a sign.

"Let's hear what you make of me," he said.

When Dawney had examined him, he asked:

"Well?"

"Well," answered Dawney slowly, "there's trouble, of course."

Mr. Treffry broke out with a husky whisper: "Out with it, Doctor; don't humbug me."

Dawney bent down, and took his wrist.

"I don't know how you've got into this state, sir," he said with the brusqueness of emotion. "You're in a bad way. It's the old trouble; and you know what that means as well as I. All I can tell you is, I'm going to have a big fight with it. It shan't be my fault, there's my hand on that."

Mr. Treffry lay with his eyes fixed on the ceiling; at last he said:

"I want to live."

"Yes—yes."

"I feel better now; don't make a fuss about it. It'll be very awkward if I die just now. Patch me up, for the sake of my niece."

Dawney nodded. "One minute, there are a few things I want," and he went out.

A moment later Greta stole in on tiptoe. She bent over till her hair touched Mr. Treffry's face.

"Uncle Nic!" she whispered. He opened his eyes.

"Hallo, Greta!"

"I have come to bring you my love, Uncle Nic, and to say good-bye. Papa says that I and Scruff and Miss Naylor are going to Vienna with him; we have had to pack in half an hour; in five minutes we are going to Vienna, and it is my first visit there, Uncle Nic."

"To Vienna!" Mr. Treffry repeated slowly. "Don't have a guide, Greta; they're humbugs."

"No, Uncle Nic," said Greta solemnly.

"Draw the curtains, old girl, let's have a look at you. Why, you're as smart as ninepence!"

"Yes," said Greta with a sigh, touching the buttons of her cape, "because I am going to Vienna; but I am sorry to leave you, Uncle Nic."

"Are you, Greta?"

"But you will have Chris, and you are fonder of Chris than of me, Uncle Nic."

"I've known her longer."

"Perhaps when you've known me as long as Chris, you shall be as fond of me."

"When I've known you as long—may be."

"While I am gone, Uncle Nic, you are to get well, you are not very well, you know."

"What put that into your head?"

"If you were well you would be smoking a cigar—it is just three o'clock. This kiss is for myself, this is for Scruff, and this is for Miss Naylor."

She stood upright again; a tremulous, joyful gravity was in her eyes and on her lips.

"Good-bye, my dear; take care of yourselves; and don't you have a guide, they're humbugs."

"No, Uncle Nic. There is the carriage! To Vienna, Uncle Nic!" The dead gold of her hair gleamed in the doorway. Mr. Treffry raised himself upon his elbow.

"Give us one more, for luck!"

Greta ran back.

"I love you very much!" she said, and kissing him, backed slowly, then, turning, flew out like a bird.

Mr. Treffry fixed his eyes on the shut door.

XXI

After many days of hot, still weather, the wind had come, and whirled the dust along the parched roads. The leaves were all astir, like tiny wings. Round Villa Rubein the pigeons cooed uneasily, all the other birds were silent. Late in the afternoon Christian came out on the veranda, reading a letter:

"DEAR CHRIS, We are here now six days, and it is a very large place with many churches. In the first place then we have been to a great many, but the nicest of them is not St. Stephan's Kirche, it is another, but I do not remember the name. Papa is out nearly all the night; he says he is resting here, so he is not able to come to the churches with us, but I do not think he rests very much. The day before yesterday we, that is, Papa, I, and Miss Naylor, went to an exhibition of pictures. It was quite beautiful and interesting (Miss Naylor says it is not right to say 'quite' beautiful, but I do not know what other word could mean 'quite' except the word 'quite,' because it is not exceedingly and not extremely). And O Chris! there was one picture painted by him; it was about a ship without masts—Miss Naylor says it is a barge, but I do not know what a barge is—on fire, and, floating down a river in a fog. I think it is extremely beautiful. Miss Naylor says it is very impressionistick—what is that? and Papa said 'Puh!' but he did not know it was painted by Herr Harz, so I did not tell him.

"There has also been staying at our hotel that Count Sarelli who came one evening to dinner at our house, but he is gone away now. He sat all day in the winter garden reading, and at night he went out with Papa. Miss Naylor says he is unhappy, but I think he does not take enough exercise; and O Chris! one day he said to me, 'That is your sister, Mademoiselle, that young lady in the white dress? Does she always wear white dresses?' and I said to him: 'It is not always a white dress; in the picture, it is green, because the picture is called 'Spring.' But I did not tell him the colours of all your dresses because he looked so tired. Then he said to me: 'She is very charming.' So I tell you this, Chris, because I think you shall like to know. Scruff' has a sore toe; it is because he has eaten too much meat.

"It is not nice without you, Chris, and Miss Naylor says I am improving my mind here, but I do not think it shall improve very much, because at night I like it always best, when the shops are lighted and the carriages are driving past; then I am wanting to dance. The first night Papa said he would take me to the theatre, but yesterday he said it was not good for me; perhaps to-morrow he shall think it good for me again.

"Yesterday we have been in the Prater, and saw many people, and some that Papa knew; and then came the most interesting part of all, sitting under the trees in the rain for two hours because we could not get a carriage (very exciting).

"There is one young lady here, only she is not any longer very young, who knew Papa when he was a boy. I like her very much; she shall soon know me quite to the bottom and is very kind.

"The ill husband of Cousin Teresa who went with us to Meran and lost her umbrella and Dr. Edmund was so sorry about it, has been very much worse, so she is not here but in Baden. I wrote to her but have no news, so I do not know whether he is still living or not, at any rate he can't get well again so soon (and I don't think he ever shall). I think as the weather is very warm you and Uncle Nic are sitting much out of doors. I am sending presents to you all in a wooden box and screwed very firm, so you shall have to use again the big screw-driver of Fritz. For Aunt Constance, photographs; for Uncle Nic, a green bird on a stand with a hole in the back of the bird to put his ashes in; it is a good green and not expensif please tell him, because he does not like expensif presents (Miss Naylor says the bird has an inquiring eye—it is a parrat); for you, a little brooch of turquoise because I like them best; for Dr. Edmund a machine to weigh medicines in because he said he could not get a good one in Botzen; this is a very good one, the shopman told me so, and is the most expensif of all the presents—so that is all my money, except two gulden. If Papa shall give me some more, I shall buy for Miss Naylor a parasol, because it is useful and the handle of hers is 'wobbley' (that is one of Dr. Edmund's words and I like it).

"Good-bye for this time. Greta sends you her kiss.

"P. S.—Miss Naylor has read all this letter (except about the parasol) and there are several things she did not want me to put, so I have copied it without the things, but at the last I have kept that copy myself, so that is why this is smudgy and several words are not spelt well, but all the things are here."

Christian read, smiling, but to finish it was like dropping a talisman, and her face clouded. A sudden draught blew her hair about, and from within, Mr. Treffry's cough mingled with the soughing of the wind; the sky was fast blackening. She went indoors, took a pen and began to write:

"MY FRIEND, Why haven't you written to me? It is so, long to wait. Uncle says you are in Italy—it is dreadful not to know for certain. I feel you would have written if you could; and I can't help thinking of all the things that may have happened. I am unhappy. Uncle Nic is ill; he will not confess it, that is his way; but he is very ill. Though perhaps you will never see this, I must write down all my thoughts. Sometimes I feel that I am brutal to be always thinking about you, scheming how to be with you again, when he is lying there so ill. How good he has always been to me; it is terrible that love should pull one apart so. Surely love should be beautiful, and peaceful, instead of filling me with bitter, wicked thoughts. I love you—and I love him; I feel as if I were torn in two. Why should it be so? Why should the beginning of one life mean the ending of another, one love the destruction of another? I don't understand. The same spirit makes me love you and him, the same sympathy, the same trust— yet it sometimes seems as if I were a criminal in loving you. You know what he thinks—he is too honest not to have shown you. He has talked to me; he likes you in a way, but you are a foreigner— he says-your life is not my life. 'He is not the man for you!' Those were his words. And now he doesn't talk to me, but when I am in the room he looks at me—that's worse—a thousand times; when he talks it rouses me to fight—when it's his eyes only, I'm a coward at once; I feel I would do anything, anything, only not to hurt him. Why can't he see? Is it because he's old and we are young? He may consent, but he will never, never see; it will always hurt him.

"I want to tell you everything; I have had worse thoughts than these—sometimes I have thought that I should never have the courage to face the struggle which you have to face. Then I feel quite broken; it is like something giving way in me. Then I think of you, and it is over; but it has been there, and I am ashamed—I told you I was a coward. It's like the feeling one would have going out into a storm on a dark night, away from a warm fire—only of the spirit not the body—which makes it worse. I had to tell you this; you mustn't think of it again, I mean to fight it away and forget that it has ever been there. But Uncle Nic—what am I to do? I hate myself because I am young, and he is old and weak—sometimes I seem even to hate him. I have all sorts of thoughts, and always at the end of them, like a dark hole at the end of a passage, the thought that I ought to give you up. Ought I? Tell me. I want to know, I want to do what is right; I still want to do that, though sometimes I think I am all made of evil.

"Do you remember once when we were talking, you said: 'Nature always has an answer for every question; you cannot get an answer from laws, conventions, theories, words, only from Nature.' What do you say to me now; do you tell me it is Nature to come to you in spite of everything, and so, that it must be right? I think you would; but can it be Nature to do something which will hurt terribly one whom I love and who loves me? If it is—Nature is cruel. Is that one of the 'lessons of life'? Is that what Aunt Constance means when she says: 'If life were not a paradox, we could not get on at all'? I am beginning to see that everything has its dark side; I never believed that before.

"Uncle Nic dreads the life for me; he doesn't understand (how should he?—he has always had money) how life can be tolerable without money—it is horrible that the accident of money should make such difference in our lives. I am sometimes afraid myself, and I can't outface that fear in him; he sees the shadow of his fear in me—his eyes seem to see everything that is in me now; the eyes of old people are the saddest things in the world. I am writing like a wretched coward, but you will never see this letter I suppose, and so it doesn't matter; but if you do, and I pray that you may—well, if I am only worth taking at my best, I am not worth taking at all. I want you to know the worst of me—you, and no one else.

"With Uncle Nic it is not as with my stepfather; his opposition only makes me angry, mad, ready to do anything, but with Uncle Nic I feel so bruised—so sore. He said: 'It is not so much the money, because there is always mine.' I could never do a thing he cannot bear, and take his money, and you would never let me. One knows very little of anything in the world till trouble comes. You know how it is with flowers and trees; in the early spring they look so quiet and self-contained; then all in a moment they change—I think it must be like that with the heart. I used to think I knew a great deal, understood why and how things came about; I thought self-possession and reason so easy; now I know nothing. And nothing in the world matters but to see you and hide away from that look in Uncle Nic's eyes. Three months ago I did not know you, now I write like this. Whatever I look at, I try to see as you would see; I feel, now you are away even more than when you were with me, what your thoughts would be, how you would feel about this or that. Some things you have said seem always in my mind like lights—"

A slanting drift of rain was striking the veranda tiles with a cold, ceaseless hissing. Christian shut the window, and went into her uncle's room.

He was lying with closed eyes, growling at Dominique, who moved about noiselessly, putting the room ready for the night. When he had finished, and with a compassionate bow had left the room, Mr. Treffry opened his eyes, and said:

"This is beastly stuff of the doctor's, Chris, it puts my monkey up; I can't help swearing after I've taken it; it's as beastly as a vulgar woman's laugh, and I don't know anything beastlier than that!"

"I have a letter from Greta, Uncle Nic; shall I read it?"

He nodded, and Christian read the letter, leaving out the mention of Harz, and for some undefined reason the part about Sarelli.

"Ay!" said Mr. Treffry with a feeble laugh, "Greta and her money! Send her some more, Chris. Wish I were a youngster again; that's a beast of a proverb about a dog and his day. I'd like to go fishing again in the West Country! A fine time we had when we were youngsters. You don't get such times these days. 'Twasn't often the fishing-smacks went out without us. We'd watch their lights from our bedroom window; when they were swung aboard we were out and down to the quay before you could say 'knife.' They always waited for us; but your Uncle Dan was the favourite, he was the chap for luck. When I get on my legs, we might go down there, you and I? For a bit, just to see? What d'you say, old girl?"

Their eyes met.

"I'd like to look at the smack lights going to sea on a dark night; pity you're such a duffer in a boat— we might go out with them. Do you a power of good! You're not looking the thing, my dear."

His voice died wistfully, and his glance, sweeping her face, rested on her hands, which held and twisted Greta's letter. After a minute or two of silence he boomed out again with sudden energy:

"Your aunt'll want to come and sit with me, after dinner; don't let her, Chris, I can't stand it. Tell her I'm asleep—the doctor'll be here directly; ask him to make up some humbug for you—it's his business."

He was seized by a violent fit of pain which seemed to stab his breath away, and when it was over signed that he would be left alone. Christian went back to her letter in the other room, and had written these words, when the gong summoned her to dinner:

"I'm like a leaf in the wind, I put out my hand to one thing, and it's seized and twisted and flung aside. I want you—I want you; if I could see you I think I should know what to do—"

XXII

The rain drove with increasing fury. The night was very black. Nicholas Treffry slept heavily. By the side of his bed the night-lamp cast on to the opposite wall a bright disc festooned by the hanging shadow of the ceiling. Christian was leaning over him. For the moment he filled all her heart, lying there, so helpless. Fearful of waking him she slipped into the sitting-room. Outside the window stood a man with his face pressed to the pane. Her heart thumped; she went up and unlatched the window. It was Harz, with the rain dripping off him. He let fall his hat and cape.

"You!" she said, touching his sleeve. "You! You!"

He was sodden with wet, his face drawn and tired; a dark growth of beard covered his cheeks and chin.

"Where is your uncle?" he said; "I want to see him."

She put her hand up to his lips, but he caught it and covered it with kisses.

"He's asleep—ill—speak gently!"

"I came to him first," he muttered.

Christian lit the lamp; and he looked at her hungrily without a word.

"It's not possible to go on like this; I came to tell your uncle so. He is a man. As for the other, I want to have nothing to do with him! I came back on foot across the mountains. It's not possible to go on like this, Christian."

She handed him her letter. He held it to the light, clearing his brow of raindrops. When he had read to the last word he gave it her back, and whispered: "Come!"

Her lips moved, but she did not speak.

"While this goes on I can't work; I can do nothing. I can't—I won't bargain with my work; if it's to be that, we had better end it. What are we waiting for? Sooner or later we must come to this. I'm sorry that he's ill, God knows! But that changes nothing. To wait is tying me hand and foot—it's making me afraid! Fear kills! It will kill you! It kills work, and I must work, I can't waste time—I won't! I will sooner give you up." He put his hands on her shoulders. "I love you! I want you! Look in my eyes and see if you dare hold back!"

Christian stood with the grip of his strong hands on her shoulders, without a movement or sign. Her face was very white. And suddenly he began to kiss that pale, still face, to kiss its eyes and lips, to kiss it from its chin up to its hair; and it stayed pale, as a white flower, beneath those kisses—as a white flower, whose stalk the fingers bend back a little.

There was a sound of knocking on the wall; Mr. Treffry called feebly. Christian broke away from Harz.

"To-morrow!" he whispered, and picking up his hat and cloak, went out again into the rain.

XXIII

It was not till morning that Christian fell into a troubled sleep. She dreamed that a voice was calling her, and she was filled with a helpless, dumb dream terror.

When she woke the light was streaming in; it was Sunday, and the cathedral bells were chiming. Her first thought was of Harz. One step, one moment of courage! Why had she not told her uncle? If he had only asked! But why—why should she tell him? When it was over and she was gone, he would see that all was for the best.

Her eyes fell on Greta's empty bed. She sprang up, and bending over, kissed the pillow. 'She will mind at first; but she's so young! Nobody will really miss me, except Uncle Nic!' She stood along while in the window without moving. When she was dressed she called out to her maid:

"Bring me some milk, Barbi; I'm going to church."

"Ach! gnadiges Fraulein, will you no breakfast have?"

"No thank you, Barbi."

"Liebes Fraulein, what a beautiful morning after the rain it has become! How cool! It is for you good—for the colour in your cheeks; now they will bloom again!" and Barbi stroked her own well-coloured cheeks.

Dominique, sunning himself outside with a cloth across his arm, bowed as she passed, and smiled affectionately:

"He is better this morning, M'mselle. We march—we are getting on. Good news will put the heart into you."

Christian thought: 'How sweet every one is to-day!'

Even the Villa seemed to greet her, with the sun aslant on it; and the trees, trembling and weeping golden tears. At the cathedral she was early for the service, but here and there were figures on their knees; the faint, sickly odour of long-burnt incense clung in the air; a priest moved silently at the far end. She knelt, and when at last she rose the service had begun. With the sound of the intoning a sense of peace came to her—the peace of resolution. For good or bad she felt that she had faced her fate.

She went out with a look of quiet serenity and walked home along the dyke. Close to Harz's studio she sat down. Now—it was her own; all that had belonged to him, that had ever had a part in him.

An old beggar, who had been watching her, came gently from behind. "Gracious lady!" he said, peering at her eyes, "this is the lucky day for you. I have lost my luck."

Christian opened her purse, there was only one coin in it, a gold piece; the beggar's eyes sparkled.

She thought suddenly: 'It's no longer mine; I must begin to be careful,' but she felt ashamed when she looked at the old man.

"I am sorry," she said; "yesterday I would have given you this, but—but now it's already given."

He seemed so old and poor—what could she give him? She unhooked a little silver brooch at her throat. "You will get something for that," she said; "it's better than nothing. I am very sorry you are so old and poor."

The beggar crossed himself. "Gracious lady," he muttered, "may you never want!"

Christian hurried on; the rustling of leaves soon carried the words away. She did not feel inclined to go in, and crossing the bridge began to climb the hill. There was a gentle breeze, drifting the clouds across the sun; lizards darted out over the walls, looked at her, and whisked away.

The sunshine, dappling through the tops of trees, gashed down on a torrent. The earth smelt sweet, the vineyards round the white farms glistened; everything seemed to leap and dance with sap and life; it was a moment of Spring in midsummer. Christian walked on, wondering at her own happiness.

'Am I heartless?' she thought. 'I am going to leave him—I am going into life; I shall have to fight now, there'll be no looking back.'

The path broke away and wound down to the level of the torrent; on the other side it rose again, and was lost among trees. The woods were dank; she hastened home.

In her room she began to pack, sorting and tearing up old letters. 'Only one thing matters,' she thought; 'singleness of heart; to see your way, and keep to it with all your might.'

She looked up and saw Barbi standing before her with towels in her hands, and a scared face.

"Are you going a journey, gnadiges Fraulein?"

"I am going away to be married, Barbi," said Christian at last; "don't speak of it to any one, please."

Barbi leant a little forward with the towels clasped to the blue cotton bosom of her dress.

"No, no! I will not speak. But, dear Fraulein, that is a big matter; have you well thought?"

"Thought, Barbi? Have I not!"

"But, dear Fraulein, will you be rich?"

"No! I shall be as poor as you."

"Ach! dear God! that is terrible. Katrina, my sister, she is married; she tells me all her life; she tells me it is very hard, and but for the money in her stocking it would be harder. Dear Fraulein, think again! And is he good? Sometimes they are not good."

"He is good," said Christian, rising; "it is all settled!" and she kissed Barbi on the cheek.

"You are crying, liebes Fraulein! Think yet again, perhaps it is not quite all settled; it is not possible that a maiden should not a way out leave?"

Christian smiled. "I don't do things that way, Barbi."

Barbi hung the towels on the horse, and crossed herself.

XXIV

Mr. Treffry's gaze was fixed on a tortoise-shell butterfly fluttering round the ceiling. The insect seemed to fascinate him, as things which move quickly always fascinate the helpless. Christian came softly in.

"Couldn't stay in bed, Chris," he called out with an air of guilt. "The heat was something awful. The doctor piped off in a huff, just because o' this." He motioned towards a jug of claret-cup and a pipe on the table by his elbow. "I was only looking at 'em."

Christian, sitting down beside him, took up a fan.

"If I could get out of this heat—" he said, and closed his eyes.

'I must tell him,' she thought; 'I can't slink away.'

"Pour me out some of that stuff, Chris."

She reached for the jug. Yes! She must tell him! Her heart sank.

Mr. Treffry took a lengthy draught. "Broken my promise; don't matter—won't hurt any one but me." He took up the pipe and pressed tobacco into it. "I've been lying here with this pain going right through me, and never a smoke! D'you tell me anything the parsons say can do me half the good of this pipe?" He leaned back, steeped in a luxury of satisfaction. He went on, pursuing a private train of thought: "Things have changed a lot since my young days. When I was a youngster, a young fellow had to look out for peck and perch—he put the future in his pocket. He did well or not, according as he had stuff in him. Now he's not content with that, it seems—trades on his own opinion of himself; thinks he is what he says he's going to be."

"You are unjust," said Christian.

Mr. Treffry grunted. "Ah, well! I like to know where I am. If I lend money to a man, I like to know whether he's going to pay it back; I may not care whether he does or not, but I like to know. The same with other things. I don't care what a man has—though, mind you, Chris, it's not a bad rule that measures men by the balance at their banks; but when it comes to marriage, there's a very simple rule, What's not enough for one is not enough for two. You can't talk black white, or bread into your mouth. I don't care to speak about myself, as you know, Chris, but I tell you this—when I came to London I wanted to marry—I hadn't any money, and I had to want. When I had the money—but that's neither here nor there!" He frowned, fingering his pipe.

"I didn't ask her, Chris; I didn't think it the square thing; it seems that's out of fashion!"

Christian's cheeks were burning.

"I think a lot while I lie here," Mr. Treffry went on; "nothing much else to do. What I ask myself is this: What do you know about what's best for you? What do you know of life? Take it or leave it, life's not all you think; it's give and get all the way, a fair start is everything."

Christian thought: 'Will he never see?'

Mr. Treffry went on:

"I get better every day, but I can't last for ever. It's not pleasant to lie here and know that when I'm gone there'll be no one to keep a hand on the check string!"

"Don't talk like that, dear!" Christian murmured.

"It's no use blinking facts, Chris. I've lived a long time in the world; I've seen things pretty well as they are; and now there's not much left for me to think about but you."

"But, Uncle, if you loved him, as I do, you couldn't tell me to be afraid! It's cowardly and mean to be afraid. You must have forgotten!"

Mr. Treffry closed his eyes.

"Yes," he said; "I'm old."

The fan had dropped into Christian's lap; it rested on her white frock like a large crimson leaf; her eyes were fixed on it.

Mr. Treffry looked at her. "Have you heard from him?" he asked with sudden intuition.

"Last night, in that room, when you thought I was talking to Dominique—"

The pipe fell from his hand.

"What!" he stammered: "Back?"

Christian, without looking up, said:

"Yes, he's back; he wants me—I must go to him, Uncle."

There was a long silence.

"You must go to him?" he repeated.

She longed to fling herself down at his knees, but he was so still, that to move seemed impossible; she remained silent, with folded hands.

Mr. Treffry spoke:

"You'll let me know—before—you—go. Goodnight!"

Christian stole out into the passage. A bead curtain rustled in the draught; voices reached her.

"My honour is involved, or I would give the case up."

"He is very trying, poor Nicholas! He always had that peculiar quality of opposition; it has brought him to grief a hundred times. There is opposition in our blood; my family all have it. My eldest brother died of it; with my poor sister, who was as gentle as a lamb, it took the form of doing the right thing in the wrong place. It is a matter of temperament, you see. You must have patience."

"Patience," repeated Dawney's voice, "is one thing; patience where there is responsibility is another. I've not had a wink of sleep these last two nights."

There was a faint, shrill swish of silk.

"Is he so very ill?"

Christian held her breath. The answer came at last.

"Has he made his will? With this trouble in the side again, I tell you plainly, Mrs. Decie, there's little or no chance."

Christian put her hands up to her ears, and ran out into the air. What was she about to do, then—to leave him dying!

XXV

On the following day Harz was summoned to the Villa. Mr. Treffry had just risen, and was garbed in a dressing-suit, old and worn, which had a certain air of magnificence. His seamed cheeks were newly shaved.

"I hope I see you well," he said majestically.

Thinking of the drive and their last parting, Harz felt sorry and ashamed. Suddenly Christian came into the room; she stood for a moment looking at him; then sat down.

"Chris!" said Mr. Treffry reproachfully. She shook her head, and did not move; mournful and intent, her eyes seemed full of secret knowledge.

Mr. Treffry spoke:

"I've no right to blame you, Mr. Harz, and Chris tells me you came to see me first, which is what I would have expected of you; but you shouldn't have come back."

"I came back, sir, because I found I was obliged. I must speak out."

"I ask nothing better," Mr. Treffry replied.

Harz looked again at Christian; but she made no sign, sitting with her chin resting on her hands.

"I have come for her," he said; "I can make my living—enough for both of us. But I can't wait."

"Why?"

Harz made no answer.

Mr. Treffry boomed out again: "Why? Isn't she worth waiting for? Isn't she worth serving for?"

"I can't expect you to understand me," the painter said. "My art is my life to me. Do you suppose that if it wasn't I should ever have left my village; or gone through all that I've gone through, to get as far even as I am? You tell me to wait. If my thoughts and my will aren't free, how can I work? I shan't be worth my salt. You tell me to go back to England—knowing she is here, amongst you who hate me, a thousand miles away. I shall know that there's a death fight going on in her and outside her against me—you think that I can go on working under these conditions. Others may be able, I am not. That's the plain truth. If I loved her less—"

There was a silence, then Mr. Treffry said:

"It isn't fair to come here and ask what you're asking. You don't know what's in the future for you, you don't know that you can keep a wife. It isn't pleasant, either, to think you can't hold up your head in your own country."

Harz turned white.

"Ah! you bring that up again!" he broke out. "Seven years ago I was a boy and starving; if you had been in my place you would have done what I did. My country is as much to me as your country is to you. I've been an exile seven years, I suppose I shall always be I've had punishment enough; but if you think I am a rascal, I'll go and give myself up." He turned on his heel.

"Stop! I beg your pardon! I never meant to hurt you. It isn't easy for me to eat my words," Mr. Treffry said wistfully, "let that count for something." He held out his hand.

Harz came quickly back and took it. Christian's gaze was never for a moment withdrawn; she seemed trying to store up the sight of him within her. The light darting through the half-closed shutters gave her eyes a strange, bright intensity, and shone in the folds of her white dress like the sheen of birds' wings.

Mr. Treffry glanced uneasily about him. "God knows I don't want anything but her happiness," he said. "What is it to me if you'd murdered your mother? It's her I'm thinking of."

"How can you tell what is happiness to her? You have your own ideas of happiness—not hers, not mine. You can't dare to stop us, sir!"

"Dare?" said Mr. Treffry. "Her father gave her over to me when she was a mite of a little thing; I've known her all her life. I've—I've loved her—and you come here with your 'dare'!" His hand dragged at his beard, and shook as though palsied.

A look of terror came into Christian's face.

"All right, Chris! I don't ask for quarter, and I don't give it!"

Harz made a gesture of despair.

"I've acted squarely by you, sir," Mr. Treffry went on, "I ask the same of you. I ask you to wait, and come like an honest man, when you can say, 'I see my way—here's this and that for her.' What makes this art you talk of different from any other call in life? It doesn't alter facts, or give you what other men have no right to expect. It doesn't put grit into you, or keep your hands clean, or prove that two and two make five."

Harz answered bitterly:

"You know as much of art as I know of money. If we live a thousand years we shall never understand each other. I am doing what I feel is best for both of us."

Mr. Treffry took hold of the painter's sleeve.

"I make you an offer," he said. "Your word not to see or write to her for a year! Then, position or not, money or no money, if she'll have you, I'll make it right for you."

"I could not take your money."

A kind of despair seemed suddenly to seize on Mr. Nicholas Treffry. He rose, and stood towering over them.

"All my life—" he said; but something seemed to click deep down in his throat, and he sank back in his seat.

"Go!" whispered Christian, "go!" But Mr. Treffry found his voice again: "It's for the child to say. Well, Chris!"

Christian did not speak.

It was Harz who broke the silence. He pointed to Mr. Treffry.

"You know I can't tell you to come with—that, there. Why did you send for me?" And, turning, he went out.

Christian sank on her knees, burying her face in her hands. Mr. Treffry pressed his handkerchief with a stealthy movement to his mouth. It was dyed crimson with the price of his victory.

XXVI

A telegram had summoned Herr Paul from Vienna. He had started forthwith, leaving several unpaid accounts to a more joyful opportunity, amongst them a chemist's bill, for a wonderful quack medicine of which he brought six bottles.

He came from Mr. Treffry's room with tears rolling down his cheeks, saying:

"Poor Nicholas! Poor Nicholas! Il n'a pas de chance!"

It was difficult to find any one to listen; the women were scared and silent, waiting for the orders that were now and then whispered through the door. Herr Paul could not bear this silence, and talked to his servant for half an hour, till Fritz also vanished to fetch something from the town. Then in despair Herr Paul went to his room.

It was hard not to be allowed to help—it was hard to wait! When the heart was suffering, it was frightful! He turned and, looking furtively about him, lighted a cigar. Yes, it came to every one—at some time or other; and what was it, that death they talked of? Was it any worse than life? That frightful jumble people made for themselves! Poor Nicholas! After all, it was he that had the luck!

His eyes filled with tears, and drawing a penknife from his pocket, he began to stab it into the stuffing of his chair. Scruff, who sat watching the chink of light under the door, turned his head, blinked at him, and began feebly tapping with a claw.

It was intolerable, this uncertainty—to be near, and yet so far, was not endurable!

Herr Paul stepped across the room. The dog, following, threw his black-marked muzzle upwards with a gruff noise, and went back to the door. His master was holding in his hand a bottle of champagne.

Poor Nicholas! He had chosen it. Herr Paul drained a glass.

Poor Nicholas! The prince of fellows, and of what use was one? They kept him away from Nicholas!

Herr Paul's eyes fell on the terrier. "Ach! my dear," he said, "you and I, we alone are kept away!"

He drained a second glass.

What was it? This life! Froth-like that! He tossed off a third glass. Forget! If one could not help, it was better to forget!

He put on his hat. Yes. There was no room for him there! He was not wanted!

He finished the bottle, and went out into the passage. Scruff ran and lay down at Mr. Treffry's door. Herr Paul looked at him. "Ach!" he said, tapping his chest, "ungrateful hound!" And opening the front door he went out on tiptoe....

Late that afternoon Greta stole hatless through the lilac bushes; she looked tired after her night journey, and sat idly on a chair in the speckled shadow of a lime-tree.

'It is not like home,' she thought; 'I am unhappy. Even the birds are silent, but perhaps that is because it is so hot. I have never been sad like this—for it is not fancy that I am sad this time, as it is sometimes. It is in my heart like the sound the wind makes through a wood, it feels quite empty in my heart. If it is always like this to be unhappy, then I am sorry for all the unhappy things in the world; I am sorrier than I ever was before.'

A shadow fell on the grass, she raised her eyes, and saw Dawney.

"Dr. Edmund!" she whispered.

Dawney turned to her; a heavy furrow showed between his brows. His eyes, always rather close together, stared painfully.

"Dr. Edmund," Greta whispered, "is it true?"

He took her hand, and spread his own palm over it.

"Perhaps," he said; "perhaps not. We must hope."

Greta looked up, awed.

"They say he is dying."

"We have sent for the best man in Vienna."

Greta shook her head.

"But you are clever, Dr. Edmund; and you are afraid."

"He is brave," said Dawney; "we must all be brave, you know. You too!"

"Brave?" repeated Greta; "what is it to be brave? If it is not to cry and make a fuss—that I can do. But if it is not to be sad in here," she touched her breast, "that I cannot do, and it shall not be any good for me to try."

"To be brave is to hope; don't give up hope, dear."

"No," said Greta, tracing the pattern of the sunlight on her skirt. "But I think that when we hope, we are not brave, because we are expecting something for ourselves. Chris says that hope is prayer, and if it is prayer, then all the time we are hoping, we are asking for something, and it is not brave to ask for things."

A smile curved Dawney's mouth.

"Go on, Philosopher!" he said. "Be brave in your own way, it will be just as good as anybody else's."

"What are you going to do to be brave, Dr. Edmund?"

"I? Fight! If only we had five years off his life!"

Greta watched him as he walked away.

"I shall never be brave," she mourned; "I shall always be wanting to be happy." And, kneeling down, she began to disentangle a fly, imprisoned in a cobweb. A plant of hemlock had sprung up in the long grass by her feet. Greta thought, dismayed: 'There are weeds!'

It seemed but another sign of the death of joy.

'But it's very beautiful,' she thought, 'the blossoms are like stars. I am not going to pull it up. I will leave it; perhaps it will spread all through the garden; and if it does I do not care, for now things are not like they used to be and I do not, think they ever shall be again.'

XXVII

The days went by; those long, hot days, when the heat haze swims up about ten of the forenoon, and, as the sun sinks level with the mountains, melts into golden ether which sets the world quivering with sparkles.

At the lighting of the stars those sparkles die, vanishing one by one off the hillsides; evening comes flying down the valleys, and life rests under her cool wings. The night falls; and the hundred little voices of the night arise.

It was near grape-gathering, and in the heat the fight for Nicholas Treffry's life went on, day in, day out, with gleams of hope and moments of despair. Doctors came, but after the first he refused to see them.

"No," he said to Dawney—"throwing away money. If I pull through it won't be because of them."

For days together he would allow no one but Dawney, Dominique, and the paid nurse in the room.

"I can stand it better," he said to Christian, "when I don't see any of you; keep away, old girl, and let me get on with it!"

To have been able to help would have eased the tension of her nerves, and the aching of her heart. At his own request they had moved his bed into a corner so that he might face the wall. There he would lie for hours together, not speaking a word, except to ask for drink.

Sometimes Christian crept in unnoticed, and sat watching, with her arms tightly folded across her breast. At night, after Greta was asleep, she would toss from side to side, muttering feverish prayers. She spent hours at her little table in the schoolroom, writing letters to Harz that were never sent. Once she wrote these words: "I am the most wicked of all creatures—I have even wished that he may die!" A few minutes afterwards Miss Naylor found her with her head buried on her arms. Christian sprang up; tears were streaming down her cheeks. "Don't touch me!" she cried, and rushed away. Later, she stole into her uncle's room, and sank down on the floor beside the bed. She sat there silently, unnoticed all the evening. When night came she could hardly be persuaded to leave the room.

One day Mr. Treffry expressed a wish to see Herr Paul; it was a long while before the latter could summon courage to go in.

"There's a few dozen of the Gordon sherry at my Chambers, in London, Paul," Mr. Treffry said; "I'd be glad to think you had 'em. And my man, Dominique, I've made him all right in my will, but keep your eye on him; he's a good sort for a foreigner, and no chicken, but sooner or later, the women'll get hold of him. That's all I had to say. Send Chris to me."

Herr Paul stood by the bedside speechless. Suddenly he blurted out.

"Ah! my dear! Courage! We are all mortal. You will get well!" All the morning he walked about quite inconsolable. "It was frightful to see him, you know, frightful! An iron man could not have borne it."

When Christian came to him, Mr. Treffry raised himself and looked at her a long while.

His wistful face was like an accusation. But that very afternoon the news came from the sickroom that he was better, having had no pain for several hours.

Every one went about with smiles lurking in their eyes, and ready to break forth at a word. In the kitchen Barbi burst out crying, and, forgetting to toss the pan, spoiled a Kaiser-Schmarn she was making. Dominique was observed draining a glass of Chianti, and solemnly casting forth the last drops in libation. An order was given for tea to be taken out under the acacias, where it was always cool; it was felt that something in the nature of high festival was being held. Even Herr Paul was present; but Christian did not come. Nobody spoke of illness; to mention it might break the spell.

Miss Naylor, who had gone into the house, came back, saying:

"There is a strange man standing over there by the corner of the house."

"Really!" asked Mrs. Decie; "what does he want?"

Miss Naylor reddened. "I did not ask him. I—don't—know—whether he is quite respectable. His coat is buttoned very close, and he—doesn't seem—to have a—collar."

"Go and see what he wants, dear child," Mrs. Decie said to Greta.

"I don't know—I really do not know—" began Miss Naylor; "he has very—high—boots," but Greta was already on her way, with hands clasped behind her, and demure eyes taking in the stranger's figure.

"Please?" she said, when she was close to him.

The stranger took his cap off with a jerk.

"This house has no bells," he said in a nasal voice; "it has a tendency to discourage one."

"Yes," said Greta gravely, "there is a bell, but it does not ring now, because my uncle is so ill."

"I am very sorry to hear that. I don't know the people here, but I am very sorry to hear that.

"I would be glad to speak a few words to your sister, if it is your sister that I want."

And the stranger's face grew very red.

"Is it," said Greta, "that you are a friend of Herr Harz? If you are a friend of his, you will please come and have some tea, and while you are having tea I will look for Chris."

Perspiration bedewed the stranger's forehead.

"Tea? Excuse me! I don't drink tea."

"There is also coffee," Greta said.

The stranger's progress towards the arbour was so slow that Greta arrived considerably before him.

"It is a friend of Herr Harz," she whispered; "he will drink coffee. I am going to find Chris."

"Greta!" gasped Miss Naylor.

Mrs. Decie put up her hand.

"Ah!" she said, "if it is so, we must be very nice to him for Christian's sake."

Miss Naylor's face grew soft.

"Ah, yes!" she said; "of course."

"Bah!" muttered Herr Paul, "that recommences.'

"Paul!" murmured Mrs. Decie, "you lack the elements of wisdom."

Herr Paul glared at the approaching stranger.

Mrs. Decie had risen, and smilingly held out her hand.

"We are so glad to know you; you are an artist too, perhaps? I take a great interest in art, and especially in that school which Mr. Harz represents."

The stranger smiled.

"He is the genuine article, ma'am," he said. "He represents no school, he is one of that kind whose corpses make schools."

"Ah!" murmured Mrs. Decie, "you are an American. That is so nice. Do sit down! My niece will soon be here."

Greta came running back.

"Will you come, please?" she said. "Chris is ready."

Gulping down his coffee, the stranger included them all in a single bow, and followed her.

"Ach!" said Herr Paul, "garcon tres chic, celui-la!"

Christian was standing by her little table. The stranger began.

"I am sending Mr. Harz's things to England; there are some pictures here. He would be glad to have them."

A flood of crimson swept over her face.

"I am sending them to London," the stranger repeated; "perhaps you could give them to me to-day."

"They are ready; my sister will show you."

Her eyes seemed to dart into his soul, and try to drag something from it. The words rushed from her lips:

"Is there any message for me?"

The stranger regarded her curiously.

"No," he stammered, "no! I guess not. He is well.... I wish...." He stopped; her white face seemed to flash scorn, despair, and entreaty on him all at once. And turning, she left him standing there.

XXVIII

When Christian went that evening to her uncle's room he was sitting up in bed, and at once began to talk. "Chris," he said, "I can't stand this dying by inches. I'm going to try what a journey'll do for me. I want to get back to the old country. The doctor's promised. There's a shot in the locker yet! I believe in that young chap; he's stuck to me like a man.... It'll be your birthday, on Tuesday, old girl, and you'll be twenty. Seventeen years since your father died. You've been a lot to me.... A parson came here today. That's a bad sign. Thought it his duty! Very civil of him! I wouldn't see him, though. If there's anything in what they tell you, I'm not going to sneak in at this time o' day. There's one thing that's rather badly on my mind. I took advantage of Mr. Harz with this damned pitifulness of mine. You've a right to look at me as I've seen you sometimes when you thought I was asleep. If I hadn't been ill he'd never have left you. I don't blame you, Chris—not I! You love me? I know that, my dear. But one's alone when it comes to the run-in. Don't cry! Our minds aren't Sunday-school books; you're finding it out, that's all!" He sighed and turned away.

The noise of sun-blinds being raised vibrated through the house. A feeling of terror seized on the girl; he lay so still, and yet the drawing of each breath was a fight. If she could only suffer in his place! She went close, and bent over him.

"It's air we want, both you and I!" he muttered. Christian beckoned to the nurse, and stole out through the window.

A regiment was passing in the road; she stood half-hidden amongst the lilac bushes watching. The poplar leaves drooped lifeless and almost black above her head, the dust raised by the soldiers' feet hung in the air; it seemed as if in all the world no freshness and no life were stirring. The tramp of feet died away. Suddenly within arm's length of her a man appeared, his stick shouldered like a sword. He raised his hat.

"Good-evening! You do not remember me? Sarelli. Pardon! You looked like a ghost standing there. How badly those fellows marched! We hang, you see, on the skirts of our profession and criticise; it is all we are fit for." His black eyes, restless and malevolent like a swan's, seemed to stab her face. "A fine evening! Too hot. The storm is wanted; you feel that? It is weary waiting for the storm; but after the storm, my dear young lady, comes peace." He smiled, gently, this time, and baring his head again, was lost to view in the shadow of the trees.

His figure had seemed to Christian like the sudden vision of a threatening, hidden force. She thrust out her hands, as though to keep it off.

No use; it was within her, nothing could keep it away! She went to Mrs. Decie's room, where her aunt and Miss Naylor were conversing in low tones. To hear their voices brought back the touch of this world of everyday which had no part or lot in the terrifying powers within her.

Dawney slept at the Villa now. In the dead of night he was awakened by a light flashed in his eyes. Christian was standing there, her face pale and wild with terror, her hair falling in dark masses on her shoulders.

"Save him! Save him!" she cried. "Quick! The bleeding!"

He saw her muffle her face in her white sleeves, and seizing the candle, leaped out of bed and rushed away.

The internal haemorrhage had come again, and Nicholas Treffry wavered between life and death. When it had ceased, he sank into a sort of stupor. About six o'clock he came back to consciousness; watching his eyes, they could see a mental struggle taking place within him. At last he singled Christian out from the others by a sign.

"I'm beat, Chris," he whispered. "Let him know, I want to see him."

His voice grew a little stronger. "I thought that I could see it through—but here's the end." He lifted his hand ever so little, and let it fall again. When told a little later that a telegram had been sent to Harz his eyes expressed satisfaction.

Herr Paul came down in ignorance of the night's events. He stopped in front of the barometer and tapped it, remarking to Miss Naylor: "The glass has gone downstairs; we shall have cool weather—it will still go well with him!"

When, with her brown face twisted by pity and concern, she told him that it was a question of hours, Herr Paul turned first purple, then pale, and sitting down, trembled violently. "I cannot believe it," he exclaimed almost angrily. "Yesterday he was so well! I cannot believe it! Poor Nicholas! Yesterday he spoke to me!" Taking Miss Naylor's hand, he clutched it in his own. "Ah!" he cried, letting it go suddenly, and striking at his forehead, "it is too terrible; only yesterday he spoke to me of sherry. Is there nobody, then, who can do good?"

"There is only God," replied Miss Naylor softly.

"God?" said Herr Paul in a scared voice.

"We—can—all—pray to Him," Miss Naylor murmured; little spots of colour came into her cheeks. "I am going to do it now."

Herr Paul raised her hand and kissed it.

"Are you?" he said; "good! I too." He passed through his study door, closed it carefully behind him, then for some unknown reason set his back against it. Ugh! Death! It came to all! Some day it would come to him. It might come tomorrow! One must pray!

The day dragged to its end. In the sky clouds had mustered, and, crowding close on one another, clung round the sun, soft, thick, greywhite, like the feathers on a pigeon's breast. Towards evening faint tremblings were felt at intervals, as from the shock of immensely distant earthquakes.

Nobody went to bed that night, but in the morning the report was the same: "Unconscious—a question of hours." Once only did he recover consciousness, and then asked for Harz. A telegram had come from him, he was on the way. Towards seven of the evening the long-expected storm broke in a sky like ink. Into the valleys and over the crests of mountains it seemed as though an unseen hand were spilling goblets of pale wine, darting a sword-blade zigzag over trees, roofs, spires, peaks, into the very firmament, which answered every thrust with great bursts of groaning. Just beyond the veranda Greta saw a glowworm shining, as it might be a tiny bead of the fallen lightning. Soon the rain covered everything. Sometimes a jet of light brought the hilltops, towering, dark, and hard, over the house, to disappear again behind the raindrops and shaken leaves. Each breath drawn by the storm was like the clash of a thousand cymbals; and in his room Mr. Treffry lay unconscious of its fury.

Greta had crept in unobserved; and sat curled in a corner, with Scruff in her arms, rocking slightly to and fro. When Christian passed, she caught her skirt, and whispered: "It is your birthday, Chris!"

Mr. Treffry stirred.

"What's that? Thunder?—it's cooler. Where am I? Chris!"

Dawney signed for her to take his place.

"Chris!" Mr. Treffry said. "It's near now." She bent across him, and her tears fell on his forehead.

"Forgive!" she whispered; "love me!"

He raised his finger, and touched her cheek.

For an hour or more he did not speak, though once or twice he moaned, and faintly tightened his pressure on her fingers. The storm had died away, but very far off the thunder was still muttering.

His eyes opened once more, rested on her, and passed beyond, into that abyss dividing youth from age, conviction from conviction, life from death.

At the foot of the bed Dawney stood covering his face; behind him Dominique knelt with hands held upwards; the sound of Greta's breathing, soft in sleep, rose and fell in the stillness.

XXIX

One afternoon in March, more than three years after Mr. Treffry's death, Christian was sitting at the window of a studio in St. John's Wood. The sky was covered with soft, high clouds, through which shone little gleams of blue. Now and then a bright shower fell, sprinkling the trees, where every twig was curling upwards as if waiting for the gift of its new leaves. And it seemed to her that the boughs thickened and budded under her very eyes; a great concourse of sparrows had gathered on those boughs, and kept raising a shrill chatter. Over at the far side of the room Harz was working at a picture.

On Christian's face was the quiet smile of one who knows that she has only to turn her eyes to see what she wishes to see; of one whose possessions are safe under her hand. She looked at Harz with that possessive smile. But as into the brain of one turning in his bed grim fancies will suddenly leap up out of warm nothingness, so there leaped into her mind the memory of that long ago dawn, when he had found her kneeling by Mr. Treffry's body. She seemed to see again the dead face, so gravely quiet, and furrowless. She seemed to see her lover and herself setting forth silently along the river wall where they had first met; sitting down, still silent, beneath the poplar-tree where the little bodies of the chafers had lain strewn in the Spring. To see the trees changing from black to grey, from grey to green, and in the dark sky long white lines of cloud, lighting to the south like birds; and, very far away, rosy peaks watching the awakening of the earth. And now once again, after all that time, she felt her spirit shrink away from his; as it had shrunk in that hour, when she had seemed hateful to herself. She remembered the words she had spoken: "I have no heart left. You've torn it in two between you. Love is all self—I wanted him to die." She remembered too the raindrops on the vines like a million tiny lamps, and the throstle that began singing. Then, as dreams die out into warm nothingness, recollection vanished, and the smile came back to her lips.

She took out a letter.

"....O Chris! We are really coming; I seem to be always telling it to myself, and I have told Scruff many times, but he does not care, because he is getting old. Miss Naylor says we shall arrive for breakfast, and that we shall be hungry, but perhaps she will not be very hungry, if it is rough. Papa said to me: 'Je serai inconsolable, mais inconsolable!' But I think he will not be, because he is going to Vienna. When we are come, there will be nobody at Villa Rubein; Aunt Constance has gone a fortnight ago to Florence. There is a young man at her hotel; she says he will be one of the greatest playwriters in England, and she sent me a play of his to read; it was only a little about love, I did not like it very much.... O Chris! I think I shall cry when I see you. As I am quite grown up, Miss Naylor is not to come back with me; sometimes she is sad, but she will be glad to see you, Chris. She seems always sadder when it is Spring. Today I walked along the wall; the little green balls of wool are growing on the poplars already, and I saw one chafer; it will not be long before the cherry blossom comes; and I felt so funny, sad and happy together, and once I thought that I had wings and could fly away up the valley to Meran—but I had none, so I sat on the bench where we sat the day we took the pictures, and I thought and thought; there was nothing came to me in my thoughts, but all was sweet and a little noisy, and rather sad; it was like the buzzing of the chafer, in my head; and now I feel so tired and all my blood is running up and down me. I do not mind, because I know it is the Spring.

"Dominique came to see us the other day; he is very well, and is half the proprietor of the Adler Hotel, at Meran; he is not at all different, and he asked about you and about Alois—do you know, Chris, to myself I call him Herr Harz, but when I have seen him this time I shall call him Alois in my heart also.

"I have a letter from Dr. Edmund; he is in London, so perhaps you have seen him, only he has a great many patients and some that he has 'hopes of killing soon'! especially one old lady, because she is always wanting him to do things for her, and he is never saying 'No,' so he does not like her. He says that he is getting old. When I have finished this letter I am going to write and tell him that perhaps he shall see me soon, and then I think he will be very sad. Now that the Spring is come there are more flowers to take to Uncle Nic's grave, and every day, when I am gone, Barbi is to take them so that he shall not miss you, Chris, because all the flowers I put there are for you.

"I am buying some toys without paint on for my niece.

"O Chris! this will be the first baby that I have known.

"I am only to stay three weeks with you, but I think when I am once there I shall be staying longer. I send a kiss for my niece, and to Herr Harz, my love—that is the last time I shall call him Herr Harz; and to you, Chris, all the joy that is in my heart.—Your loving

"GRETA."

Christian rose, and, turning very softly, stood, leaning her elbows on the back of a high seat, looking at her husband.

In her eyes there was a slow, clear, faintly smiling, yet yearning look, as though this strenuous figure bent on its task were seen for a moment as something apart, and not all the world to her.

"Tired?" asked Harz, putting his lips to her hand.

"No, it's only—what Greta says about the Spring; it makes one want more than one has got."

Slipping her hand away, she went back to the window. Harz stood, looking after her; then, taking up his palette, again began painting.

In the world, outside, the high soft clouds flew by; the trees seemed thickening and budding.

And Christian thought:

'Can we never have quite enough?'

December 1890.

John Galsworthy – His Life And Times

John Galsworthy, eldest son of John Galsworthy (1817-1904), a solicitor and company director of Old Jewry, London, and Blanche Bailey (1835-1915), daughter of Charles Bartleet, a needlemaker in Redditch. His father's ancestors originated in Wembury, near Plymouth in England, and Galsworthy, for whom family origins were of significant importance, maintained a close connection with Devon. His more immediate family were considerably wealthy and well established in the shipping industry, and owned a fine estate in Kingston-upon-Thames called Parkfield, where Galsworthy was born on the 14th August 1867. At the age of nine he began education at Saugeen, a Bournemouth preparatory school, before starting at Harrow school in 1881 where he remained until 1886, distinguishing himself as an athlete.

His education at Harrow being successful enough to gain him entrance to Oxford, he began at New College to read law and gained a second-class degree with honours in 1889. Following Lincoln's Inn he was called to the bar in 1890. Despite this recognition he realised that he was not keen to actually begin practising law and so he resolved instead to look after the family's shipping business while specialising himself in Marine Law. This decision saw him take to the seas to destinations such as Vancouver, Island and South AFrica, though it was at the age of twenty-five on one particular journey to Australia, motivated by an (unfulfilled) intention to meet Robert Louis Stevenson on Samoa that he would being to realise fully his literary interests: though he was not considering becoming a writer at this time, his enjoyment of literature was enough to encourage an attempt at meeting a great writer and eventually enabled one of the most significant encounters of his life. He made the journey with his friend Edward Sanderson and, though he missed Stevenson, he met Joseph Conrad, a fellow future author famed for his novels which were often nautically themed. At the time Conrad was the first mate of the sailing-ship Torrens moored in the harbour of Adelaide, Australia; still very much focused on his ship-borne career, he was yet to begin his writing in earnest.

Indeed, though neither knew at the time, both Conrad and Galsworthy were at similar junctures in their lives, their time spent as sea acting as a transitional period during which each found their literary calling. It is perhaps owning to this unknown common ground that they became close friends. During his time on the Torrens Galsworthy recorded several details, offering a frank and valuable characterisation of Conrad while also illuminating his own experiences as a student of Marine Law.

"I supposed to be studying navigation for the Admiralty Bar, would every day work out the position of the ship with the captain. On one side of the saloon table we would sit and check our observations with those of Conrad, who from the other side of the table would look at us a little quizzically."

On his return to England and the cessation of his nautical voyaging, Galsworthy began an affair with the wife of his first cousin, Major Arthur John Galsworthy. Ada Nemesis Pearson Cooper (1864-1956), the daughter of Emanuel Copper, an obstetrician from Norwich, remained married to the Major for ten years and the affair remained secret for its duration. In order to conceal the affair they took considerable pains to avoid suspicion. One such tactic was to stay in a secluded farmhouse called Wingstone in the village on Manaton on Dartmoor, in Devon. In Galsworthy's decision to choose Devon as the location for their clandestine rendezvous we see evidence of Galsworthy's affection for the place of his father's origin. It was only when, in 1905, she divorced the Major that their affair became known following their marriage on 23rd September of that year.

Galsworthy now took to writing sometime after having met Conrad and his career began in earnest when, in 1897, his first work, From the Four Winds, a volume of short stories, was published under the pseudonym John Sinjohn. He succeeded this in 1898 with Jocelyn, his first novel, and then his second in 1900, Villa Rubein. In 1901 he published a second volume of short stories, A Man of Devon, which was the last of his work to be published under pseudonym. The first of his work to be published under his own name was The Island Pharisees in 1904, a novel of social observation, seasoned with flashes of satire and propaganda. His decision to write under his own name is arguably owing to the recent death of his father, either as a mark of respect to his name or because now he was able to publish freely without incurring the possibility of paternal disappointment at his choice of career. It also marked a shift in his professionalism; he had hitherto published with small, independent publishers, but The Island Pharisees was published by Heinemann, a far more established House and one with whom he remained for the duration of his writing career.

He arguably cemented his position and maturity as a writer when, in 1906, he saw the publication of both his first major play, The Silver Box, and the novel The Man of Property. Each was published to considerable critical acclaim, and to achieve both in such a short space of time was impressive. The Silver Box concerns the imbalance in the justice system with regards to criminals of differing class by contrasting the treatment of a poor thief and a rich thief, both of whom stole silver cigarette cases but for very different reasons. The complexity of individual experience when not dealt with in public is highlighted and questioned in a bravely critical manner; despite the clear issues it raises with class and privilege, the final night was attended by the Price and Princess of Wales. The Man of Property was the first novel in the famous The Forsyte Saga, a trilogy of novels with an 'interlude' between each one, written between 1906 and 1921. Dealing with the questions of status, class and materialism, The Man of Property introduces us to the Forsyte family, particularly Soames Forsyte, who is acutely aware of his status as 'new money' and equally keen to assert himself as a wealthy man. Jealous of his wife and desperate to own things in order to confirm his wealth to those observing him, he engineers a plan to keep his wife from her friends which backfires spectacularly when, instead of cutting her off, all Soames achieves is enabling her to have an affair. This drives Soames to terrible actions with terrible consequences, which Galsworthy depicts with confidence.

Very typically Edwardian, the novel focuses on conflict between property and art, and to a certain degree much of its emotional power is drawn from Galsworthy's own life, particularly his affair with Ada. Their rendezvous in the countryside of Devon mirror the manner in which Forsyte seeks to relocate his wife and; though theirs was a much healthier relationship, there are clear similarities. By examining the fragile nature of the class system and those moving within it Galsworthy offered an important perspective on the relationships between material wealth, personal happiness and obsession, and the manner in which these change over time. His contemporaries widely regarded the publication of this novel as marking the end of Victorianism. His friend Conrad praised it as "indubitably a piece of art" and, though the notoriously risqué D.H. Lawrence lamented the novel's timidity in the face of sexuality and sensuality, he considered it potentially "a very great novel, a very great satire".

Though he continued to write both plays and novels, it was his work as a playwright for which he was most celebrated by his contemporaries. Indeed, his next novel, The Country House, seems uncharacteristically unfocused, its satirical view of those belonging to the country set comparatively unremarkable and weakly characterised, while at times the tone of satire becomes one of ironic detachment. In 1909 he published Fraternity, an exploration of of the various connections between urban society and the social classes therein, though its representation of lower-class Londoners is utterly unconvincing and ill-informed. Remaining with the subject of the landed gentry and the society surrounding it, in 1915 he published The Freelands, which does not stray far from conservative discussions of capitalism, the rural economy and their interrelationship.

His drama, however, featured a convincingly muted realism, directed at a relatively small, educated and politically-aware audience. His social agenda is prevalent here too, and is represented in a simple and static manner producing arresting instances of high drama. This talent for creating moments of captivating theatre is complimented by an instinctual sense of balance enabling his narratives to vacillate between their emotional high- and low-points, ultimately reaching conclusive equilibrium. This is particularly evident in one of his most popular plays, Strife, published in 1909 and examining the antagonists in a strike at a Cornish tin mine. In this, and in 1910's Justice, he approaches his subject with sympathy, irony and balance, which establishes a position of narrative authority while garnering the audiences trust that he is representing his characters and their motives justly. Justice condemns the use of solitary confinement in prisons, a reformist agenda which caught the liberality of his contemporary audiences along with the home secretary, Winston Churchill.

Despite he was careful to disassociate himself with politics and professed himself apolitical, he and his work were nevertheless aligned with the views of the Liberal establishment. He spent much of the duration of the First World War working in a field hospital in France as an orderly having been passed over for military service.

Despite the popularity and brilliance of his work, it was only in 1920 that he had his first true commercial success with The Skin Game, a melodrama dealing with ethics, property and class. The play was adapted by Alfred Hitchcock in 1931. Galsworthy, meanwhile, had turned down a knighthood in 1918, considering his work not sufficient to be made a knight of the realm. He did, however, accept the Belgian Palmes d'Or in the following year. In 1920 he published the second novel in the Forsyte Saga, In Chancery, in which he resumes many of the themes of the first novel, focusing on the marital disharmony between Soames Forsyte and his wife. Katherine Mansfield considered it "a fascinating, brilliant book" in her review in The Atheneum. Then, in 1921, he was elected as the PEN International Literary Club's first president. The concluding novel to The Forsyte Saga, To Let was published in 1921 with a kind of peace being found between Forsyte and his now-ex wife, though he is left contemplating his losses and his greed. More ironic treatment of class confusions followed in Loyalties, bringing with it more popular success which lasted until 1926 and Escape, the last of his popular plays. Though he enjoyed popular success it was inconsistent and relatively small. His Collected Plays was published in 1929.

Over the course of time the appreciation of his work has gradually shifted from his plays to his novels, and particularly the detail and intricacy of his chronicle of English social difference, tension and pretension in The Forsyte Saga. Its success encouraged Galsworthy to revisit Soames Forsyte in a second trilogy, A Modern Comedy, which follows Soames's obsessive love of his daughter Fleur. In its three volumes, The White Monkey (1924), The Silver Spoon (1936) and Swan Song (1928) he examines the English commercial upper-middle class and its ideologies, its instinct to possess as its only way of distinguishing itself manifested in the poisonous materialism of Soames. Interestingly, this emergent social class which he so vehemently criticises is the very class from which he emerged. He witnessed first-hand its insularity, its chauvinism, its restrictive and oppressive morality, its stubborn imperialism and its materialism, and it is this experience which enables him to write so comfortably about it. Swan Song is widely considered among the best of Galsworthy's writing for the depth of its exploration of society and its heightened emotional subtlety. In 1929 he was appointed to the Order of Merit, despite having turned down a knighthood earlier. He spent his last years writing a third trilogy, End of the Chapter, beginning in 1931 with Maid in Waiting, Flowering Wilderness in 1932 and concluding with Over The River in 1933. These are significantly less coherent works and are indicative of his deteriorating health. Indeed, in 1932 he was awarded the Nobel Prize, though he was too ill to attend the ceremony.

Throughout the course of his career he received honorary degrees from the universities of St Andrews (1922), Manchester (1927), Dublin (1929), Cambridge (1930), Sheffield (1930), Oxford (1931), and Princeton (1931). In 1926 New College, Oxford, elected him as an honourary fellow. In photographs he is portrayed as handsome, fastidiously dressed and dignified. He was unusually compassionate and this saw him involved in several charitable and humane causes throughout the course of his life, including penal reforms, attacks on theatrical censorship and campaigning for animal rights. Though he spent the majority of the final seven years of his life at his home in Bury, West Sussex, it was at his home in Hampstead, London, that he died of a brain tumour on 31st January, 1933, six weeks after having been too ill to attend the ceremony in honour of his receiving the Nobel Prize. According to demands made in his will he was cremated and his ashes scattered over the South Downs from an aeroplane. Also in his will was his wish to leave cottages to several of his astonished tenants. He is memorialised in Highgate 'New' Cemetery and in the cloisters of New College, Oxford, where he was an honourary fellow.

www.ingramcontent.com/pod-product-compliance
Lightning Source LLC
Chambersburg PA
CBHW071334130626
46556CB00004B/1894

* 9 7 8 1 7 8 3 9 4 6 1 0 5 *